Praise for
Carlton M

"Easily the craziest, weirdest, strangest, funniest, most obscene writer in America."
—*GOTHIC MAGAZINE*

"Carlton Mellick III has the craziest book titles... and the kinkiest fans!"
—CHRISTOPHER MOORE, author of *The Stupidest Angel*

"If you haven't read Mellick you're not nearly perverse enough for the twenty first century."
—JACK KETCHUM, author of *The Girl Next Door*

"Carlton Mellick III is one of bizarro fiction's most talented practitioners, a virtuoso of the surreal, science fictional tale."
—CORY DOCTOROW, author of *Little Brother*

"Bizarre, twisted, and emotionally raw—Carlton Mellick's fiction is the literary equivalent of putting your brain in a blender."
—BRIAN KEENE, author of *The Rising*

"Carlton Mellick III exemplifies the intelligence and wit that lurks between its lurid covers. In a genre where crude titles are an art in themselves, Mellick is a true artist."
—*THE GUARDIAN*

"Just as Pop had Andy Warhol and Dada Tristan Tzara, the bizarro movement has its very own P. T. Barnum-type practitioner. He's the mutton-chopped author of such books as *Electric Jesus Corpse* and *The Menstruating Mall*, the illustrator, editor, and instructor of all things bizarro, and his name is Carlton Mellick III."
—*DETAILS MAGAZINE*

Also by **Carlton Mellick III**

SWEET STORY

CARLTON MELLICK III

ERASERHEAD PRESS
PORTLAND, OREGON

ERASERHEAD PRESS
PO BOX 10065
Portland, OR 97296

WWW.ERASERHEADPRESS.COM

ISBN: 978-1-62105-155-8

Printed in the USA.

AUTHOR'S NOTE

This book is not for children. Although it was written in the style of a children's book, please do not read it to your kids. If it were a movie the rating would be a hard R, maybe worse, like a Q. I'm not sure what a Q-rated story would be like but it doesn't sound like it would be very pleasant at all and I'm pretty sure it's not something you want to read to your kid.

The exception, of course, would be if you are the kind of parent who does not censor what your children read or watch no matter how depraved the content, but if you are such a person you might want to seriously reconsider your parenting methods. I was not censored as a child and look at how I turned out. I'm hardly a functioning member of society. If I wasn't somehow able to make a living writing these books I'd be the deranged man standing on your street corner selling shoes made out of marshmallows.

Is that really how you want your child to end up? Selling marshmallow shoes on a street corner and thinking sideburns with a shaved head is actually a cool hairstyle? I think not. No parent could possibly hate their child that much.

—Carlton Mellick III 6/29/2014 10:32 pm

CHAPTER ONE

Sally was told never to go to the blurry side of town. Her parents thought it was a dreadful place to venture because all the people there were always very sad and her family did not want to expose her to such sadness. On that most depressing side of town, everything appeared hazy and would never come into focus even if you wore the thickest of lenses on your glasses. Because of this constant blurriness, the people there were never able to see the beauty of the world around them. A husband could not appreciate his wife's loveliness no matter how she did her makeup or how elegant the dress she wore. A mother could not see the smiles on her children's faces, even on the rare occasions that her children did have reason to smile. They weren't able to watch television, play video games, or read books such as the book you are reading right now.

Words would never come into focus, no matter how large the font. Because of this, most children did not even bother to learn to read or write and a place where children did not write and read was a woeful place, indeed. Once these illiterate children grew to adulthood, it was impossible for them to get work at any good-paying jobs. And without good jobs they would never be able to afford to live anywhere but the blurry side of town for the rest of their lives. It was an endless cycle of misery.

Sally promised her mother and father that she would never go anywhere near the blurry side of town, but one day she couldn't help herself. The biggest, most beautiful rainbow Sally had ever seen appeared in the sky over the blurry neighborhood and Sally just had to go see it. Sally loved rainbows. She loved them even more than merry-go-rounds and strawberry ice cream sundaes. Her backpack had twelve rainbow stickers on it and she always wore rainbow socks and rainbow barrettes in her hair. And whenever she saw a rainbow appear in the sky, she would drop whatever she was doing and try to find the end of it.

Because of this, everyone always thought that Sally was a strange little girl. What kind of child runs around town all by herself chasing after rainbows? Surely it must be the act of a rather disturbed young thing who actually believed in fairies and unicorns. She was nine years old for heaven's sake. She should've been doing more mature things, such as focusing on her studies or learning to play a musical instrument such as the clarinet or the violin. Most children her age did not even believe in Santa Claus anymore and had already sold off all of their babyish toys at garage sales in order to pay for roller skates or basketball hoops or the supplies needed to start their very own lemonade business. But Sally refused to grow up. She refused to believe that magic wasn't real, no matter how old she got. If growing up meant that she could not chase after rainbows, she hoped she would stay a child forever.

"Why do you want to go to the end of the rainbow?" asked a plump little boy following Sally on his bike.

The boy was named Timmy Taco. Timmy followed Sally home from school every day. He said it was because they lived next door to each other, but it was really because he had a secret crush on her. He thought she had the prettiest black curls in her hair and the cutest pink freckles on the end of her nose.

"Because magical things always happen at the ends of rainbows," Sally said.

Sally didn't like how Timmy Taco always followed her everywhere. He was the fattest kid in school, he wore his pants too high, and his glasses were always taped together in the middle. As she walked along the sidewalk, carrying her pet turtle on her shoulder, a cool spring breeze blowing through the ruffles of her sunshine-yellow dress, she tried to walk faster to escape Timmy. Even though he was on a bicycle and could ride faster than she could walk, she hoped he would've taken the hint and left her alone.

"Like what?" Timmy asked, taking his feet off the pedals to coast down a hill.

Timmy was always on his bicycle. It was because he was too overweight and lazy to walk on his own legs. But he also didn't like to have to pedal his bike, so he tried to coast down hills as much as possible. Because the school was uphill from Timmy's house, he usually had his mother drive him to school each morning with his bike sticking out the back of the trunk. Then he'd coast down the hill on the way home. Using this tactic, the fat little boy didn't have to ever use his bike's pedals or get any exercise at all.

"Well, for starters, leprechauns live at the ends of rainbows and everyone knows that leprechauns are made of magic."

Timmy giggled at Sally for saying that.

"But leprechauns don't actually exist," Timmy said.

Sally covered her pet turtle's ears so that the little green reptile wouldn't have to hear such upsetting nonsense come from the fat little boy.

"Yes, they do. You've never been to the end of a rainbow so you don't know."

Timmy kept his mouth shut for a while. He knew better than to argue with the girl he loved.

"Well, why do you want to find a leprechaun then?" Timmy asked. "Do you think he'll give you his pot of gold?"

Sally rolled her deep blue eyes at him. "Maybe."

"Why do you want a pot of gold? Your family is already

super rich. My dad is a doctor and he doesn't even make as much as yours."

"Well, there's more than just gold at the end of the rainbow," Sally said. "Besides leprechauns, there are also fairies and unicorns that live there. If I find a magical fairy she might grant me wishes. I can wish for whatever I want."

Timmy smiled. "If we find a fairy then can I wish for whatever I want?"

Sally shook her head. "No, fairies don't like boys. Only girls can make wishes."

"Oh…" Timmy said, frowning at the sidewalk.

When they got closer to the blurry side of town, Timmy stopped his bike in Sally's path.

"You're not actually going in there, are you?"

Sally nodded her curly head. "Of course. How else will I get to see the rainbow?"

"But that's the blurry side of town. You don't want to go in there."

"If that's where the rainbow ends, that's where I need to go."

Sally tried to step around Timmy's bike, but Timmy just rolled backward into her path again. His pudgy body, even more so than the bike, made an exceptionally effective barricade.

"But what if you get lost? You won't be able to read any of the street signs in there. If you get lost on the blurry side of town, nobody will ever be able to find you again, because you'll be indistinguishable from all the other children who live there."

"I won't get lost," Sally said.

She stepped over his back wheel, getting dirt all over her pretty yellow dress. Then she continued down the sidewalk. Timmy watched as she became a blurry yellow blob the further away from him she walked.

"Wait up," Timmy said, coasting down the sidewalk toward her.

Sally realized that not even the blurry side of town would deter Timmy from pestering her.

"It's close," Sally told the Timmy-shaped blob riding up behind her. "We should hurry before it disappears."

As they walked down the sidewalk, they had to step carefully. They didn't know what all the fuzzy shapes were that they crossed. They couldn't tell a pile of dog droppings from a sleeping squirrel, or a fire hydrant from a stubby little man wearing a yellow raincoat.

"The people here are supposed to be mean and dangerous," Timmy told Sally. "We shouldn't go anywhere near them."

"They're not mean people. They're sad people. There's a difference."

"But sad people do mean things to happy people. My dad says it's because the sadness fills them with jealousy and hatred. They will hurt us and try to steal our happiness away."

Sally shook her blurry head.

"That's not true. Sad people are too sad to do anything but drink brandy and sleep all day. That's what my mom does whenever she's sad."

"Well, we should avoid them anyway. Just in case."

But the second Timmy Taco said this, they ran into a group of blurry children sitting on the sidewalk. The children were so hard to see that they didn't notice them until they almost tripped on their legs.

"Go away, you're ruining our game," said a blurry boy.

Sally and Timmy were surprised the boy sounded like a normal boy. They assumed his voice would be different, perhaps muffled and distant like the sound of talking underwater, but his voice was as clear as theirs.

"Go around, go around," said a blurry little girl.

Sally was too curious to leave right away. She leaned in close, trying to get a better view of them. But no matter how close she leaned, they remained just as blurred.

"What are you playing?" Sally asked.

"Bounces," said the blurry boy.

Sally couldn't tell how many children were there. She could tell there were at least three, but there might have been as many as six or seven. Some of the things she suspected to be other children might have just been shrubs growing along the sidewalk, however.

"What's bounces?" Sally asked.

The children laughed at her.

The blurry boy said, "Everyone knows bounces."

"How do you play?" Sally asked.

Timmy didn't like that Sally was talking to the blurry kids. The fact that he couldn't see them clearly made him twice as fearful. They could have had sharp fangs and horrible flesh-tearing claws and he wouldn't even know. Being on the blurry side of town was even scarier than sleeping without a night light.

"Come on, Sally. Let's go."

But Sally ignored the fat boy. She was curious about the blurry kids. They weren't at all what she imagined.

"Not yet," Sally said. "I want to know more about bounces."

The blurry boy oozed toward Sally and held up a big red orb that looked kind of like the oversized balls that she played kickball with at school.

He said, "You bounce the ball on the sidewalk and see how many times you can do it before it rolls away. Then you have to find it within five seconds or else you get eliminated. It's *really* hard."

Sally didn't think it seemed very hard at all. It seemed like the dumbest game she'd ever heard of.

"That doesn't seem very fun," Sally said.

"It isn't all that fun," said the blurry boy in a slightly sad voice. "But we do it for the candy."

"Candy?"

The blurry little girl said, "Yeah, whoever wins each day gets a point and whoever has the most points by the end of the year gets a piece of candy. The losers all have to chip in to buy it."

"That's it? Just one piece of candy in a whole year?"

"Have you ever had candy before?" asked the boy. "It's *really* good. I won the candy last year and can still taste it."

Timmy tugged on Sally's dress. "Come on. Don't you want to see the rainbow? It's going to disappear if we don't hurry."

But Sally wasn't listening to Timmy.

"Of course I've had candy before," Sally said. "I eat candy every day!"

The blurry kids didn't believe her.

"No you don't," said the blurry boy. "Nobody can afford to eat candy every day."

"Well, I do. My daddy buys me a piece of candy every day on his way home from work."

That's when the kids realized Sally and Timmy were not from their neighborhood.

Sally didn't need to see clearly to notice the angry expression growing on the blurry boy's face.

"You're from the clear side of town, aren't you?"

Sally shrugged but they probably couldn't tell she was shrugging.

"I'm from the normal side of town," she said.

"Let's go, Sally," Timmy said, realizing the other children were getting upset by their presence.

"We don't like clear kids," said the blurry girl. "You should go away."

"What's wrong with being clear?"

"Clear kids are spoiled selfish brats."

"No we're not," Sally said.

"Come on," Timmy said.

Now he was pulling Sally away from them.

"Yeah, go away clear kid. We don't want you."

Then the blurry kids started throwing rocks at them. Sally assumed they were rocks based on the noise they made when they hit the street. Luckily, the blurry kids weren't capable of aiming very well. All the rocks missed.

"Run!" Timmy yelled, actually pedaling his bike to get away.

The blurry kids kept yelling and throwing rocks until they were too far away to hear them anymore.

Sally and Timmy hid around a corner to catch their breath. Even though Timmy was on the bike and didn't have to run, he was twice as exhausted as Sally.

"They were so mean," Timmy said. "I told you, didn't I?"

Sally frowned and shook her head. "I don't think they were mean. They seemed sad to me."

"But they threw rocks at us!"

"Yeah, but I told them that I get candy every day and they seemed lucky if they got it even once a year. I rubbed it in their faces. I was way meaner to them than they were to me."

"Are you kidding? It's not your fault they're too poor to afford candy."

"But still, I couldn't imagine what it would be like to not have candy. It's one of my three favorite things."

"Mine too," Timmy said. "I would eat candy all day every day if my mom would let me."

"I like colorful candy. The kind that tastes like rainbows."

"There's candy that tastes like rainbows?"

"No, but if I ever took a bite of a rainbow I bet it would taste just like candy."

Timmy got excited. "Hey, maybe it does. Let's go see."

Sally looked toward the rainbow. "Let me get on the back of your bike so we can go quicker."

"Okay," Timmy said. He liked the idea of her holding on to him while they rode the bike together. "Let's go!"

But it was Sally who ended up doing all the pedaling. She sat on the front tip of the seat and pedaled the bike as Timmy hugged his sweaty stomach to her back and pressed his cheek against hers, expecting her to do all the work of lugging his plump butt down the road.

Sally didn't mind much, though, because she was able to go faster than if she were walking. It wouldn't have been an ordeal at all if her backside wasn't getting drenched in Timmy's sweat.

"I see it!" Sally said.

The rainbow came closer into view as they rode the bicycle, but there was something very odd about it. Since they were on the blurry side of town, the rainbow should have been blurry as well. But it was not blurry at all. In fact, it was more clear than it was on the clear side of town.

"What's wrong with it?" Timmy asked. "It doesn't look like a normal rainbow anymore."

The rainbow wasn't just clear. It was solid. They passed under it and the rainbow looked like an arc of stained glass hovering overhead.

Sally stopped the bike beneath to stare up at the light.

"It's so pretty," she said.

"It looks like we could walk on top of it," Timmy said.

"Yeah!" Sally said. "Let's find the end and see if we can ride the bike up the rainbow. It might bring us to a magical kingdom in the sky."

The two children road beneath the rainbow toward the end, watching it as it arched closer and closer to the ground. They were surprised that none of the other kids on that side of town cared about the rainbow. They must have been so depressed that they didn't even notice when something so beautiful was hovering above their front yard.

The rainbow ended in a deserted old park that seemed to be used more as a landfill than for picnicking or flying kites. The closer they got to the end of the rainbow, the more in focus their surroundings became. As they crossed the park, the blurriness cleared and they could see perfectly fine. But then they got even closer to the end of the rainbow and things became even more clear. They could see clearer than they could on the clear side of town. It was as though their side of town was the blurry side of town in comparison to this. Colors were brighter and textures were more distinct. Sally's yellow dress had never been as sunny and pretty as it was at that moment.

"I can't believe it," Sally said. "I'm actually going to make it to the end of the rainbow!"

"Is there a leprechaun?" Timmy asked. "You said there would be a leprechaun."

But there wasn't a leprechaun that they could see. There also wasn't a pot of gold. At the end of the rainbow, all they saw was a fat man passed out on the ground with a jug of rum in one hand and a drumstick of chicken in the other.

Sally poked the passed out drunk with a stick, poking him right in his belly that stuck out of his shirt.

"Hello?" Sally asked.

The fat drunk pushed the stick away and snored loudly. She poked him again until he woke up.

"What? What's going on?" the drunken man hollered.

"Are you a leprechaun?" Sally asked.

"Huh?" the drunk asked.

Timmy hid behind Sally. He was deathly afraid of homeless people.

"Are you a leprechaun?"

"A leprechaun?" the drunken man asked.

"Yeah," Sally said. "You're at the end of the rainbow so I thought you might be a leprechaun."

The large man stood up and wiped drool from his beard.

"Of course I'm not a leprechaun. Do I look like a leprechaun?"

Sally scanned him up and down. He didn't look anything like a leprechaun.

"Then what are you?" Sally asked.

"What am I?" the drunken man gave her an annoyed look, like he was about to slap her if she asked another stupid question. But then his face changed from grumpy to happy and a big smile grew on his face. "I'm a pirate, of course."

Then the chubby man placed a pirate hat on his head.

"A pirate?" Timmy cried.

"Pirates aren't supposed to be at the ends of rainbows," Sally said.

"They are if they're rainbow pirates," said the pirate. "And I, little lady, am the king of the rainbow pirates."

Sally frowned at the pirate. She didn't like the idea of pirates being at the end of rainbows. Leprechauns, unicorns, or fairies would all have been satisfactory. But a pirate? Stinky drunken old men had no place near rainbows, and this man was the stinkiest drunkenest man Sally had ever met. She decided that he had to be lying. He must have just been a normal homeless man pretending to be a rainbow pirate.

"If you're a pirate then where's your ship?" Sally asked.

"A ship?" the pirate said. "Rainbow pirates don't have ships. We sail across rainbows whenever we travel. Then we plunder the riches from homes within the vicinity of where the rainbow ends." The pirate looked around and scratched his chin. "But there don't seem to be many riches to be plundering around here."

"So there's no pot of gold?" Timmy asked.

"There's a treasure chest of gold," said the pirate. "But you're not getting me gold unless you can out-swashbuckle me for it." The pirate went to Timmy and leaned down at him. "And you

17

don't look like much of a swashbuckler, me boy."

Timmy shook his head. "I don't even know what a swash-buckler does."

The pirate patted him on the back. "That's good, me boy. To swashbuckle with a rainbow pirate means certain death."

Sally crossed her arms. She was very upset that the ends of rainbows were not as magical as she always thought.

"So that's it? You're not going to give us gold or wishes or anything?"

The pirate winked his bloodshot eye. "Just because I said you can't have me gold doesn't mean you don't get nothing at all, little lass. Wishes I be willing to grant."

The children's faces exploded with excitement. "Really?" they said in unison.

"Aye," said the pirate, leaning against the glowing rainbow. "You each get one wish. Anything you want."

The children looked at each other with bright faces. Then the pirate pulled out his cutlass and sliced the air between them, cutting the smiles right off their young faces.

He said, "But if you wish for more wishes I'll gut ye on the spot."

The children were so scared of the blade between their cheeks that they wondered if they should wish for anything at all.

Sally couldn't make up her mind. She thought about everything she could possibly want, but when put on the spot her mind went blank. It was too much pressure. She couldn't decide on just one wish.

"So what would you like to wish for, little girl?" the pirate asked, leaning down and spraying the girl with his horrid fishy breath.

She waved his stink away and said, "I don't know. I need to think about it."

The pirate nodded. "Aye, it's a big decision, me lass. But don't take too long. If you don't make your wish by the time the rainbow disappears, then you won't get anything at all."

"We both get wishes?" Timmy Taco asked. "We don't have to share one wish?"

The pirate nodded. "Everyone gets a wish. Even your turtle there."

Sally looked at her pet turtle sitting on her shoulder. With all that had happened, she'd completely forgotten Little Stinky was there. He sat on her shoulder so much that he was practically a part of Sally's body. Like a pirate's parrot, Stinky was her shoulder mascot.

"How will you know what Stinky wishes for?" Sally asked, stroking the turtle's shell.

"I'll ask him in turtle language," said the rainbow pirate.

The pirate leaned down and looked the turtle in the face. Then he slowly winked both eyes. The turtle closed its eyes and opened them. The pirate then winked for such a long time that it seemed like he was taking a standing nap against Sally's shoulder.

"What are you doing?" Sally asked.

"Speaking to your turtle of course," said the pirate, his eyes still closed. "They communicate very slowly."

"That's how you speak to turtles?" Timmy asked.

"Shhh!" the pirate said, concentrating on hearing the turtle's wish.

Then he winked three more times and stepped away from Stinky. "Very well. Wish granted."

"What did he wish for?" Sally asked.

The turtle leapt from Sally's shoulder and flew up into the air.

"That he could fly, of course," said the pirate.

Like he had a rocket pack as a shell, the turtle flew in circles

19

around them. A big smile spread on his little turtle face as he moved faster than any turtle ever had before.

"Look at that!" Timmy cried. "A flying turtle! A flying turtle!"

But Sally was worried Stinky might hurt himself flying through the park like that.

"It's true," Timmy said. "You really can grant wishes!"

The pirate bowed. "Of course it's true."

"So I really get a wish and it will come true?" Timmy asked. "I can really wish for anything I want?"

"Indeed, me boy."

Timmy climbed off of his bike and stepped forward. He looked at Sally, then back at the pirate.

"Then I wish..." he looked at Sally again, hesitating for a moment.

"Yes, yes, what do you want?" the pirate asked. "I don't have all day."

Then Timmy jumped up in the air. "I wish me and Sally were married forever!"

"What!" Sally cried.

"Wish granted," said the pirate.

"Wait, no!" Sally stepped between Timmy and the pirate, waving her hands.

But it was too late. A wedding ring appeared on Sally's finger and a wedding certificate appeared in Timmy's hand.

"I don't want to marry him!" Sally said, as her turtle flew around her head.

"It's too late," said the pirate. "You're already married. It is legally binding."

"I want a divorce!" Sally cried.

The pirate pointed at the wedding certificate.

"Unfortunately, you can't. This is a contract that lasts for all eternity. Divorce is impossible."

"What!" Sally was so flustered she wanted to scream.

Timmy took her by the hand and a satisfied smile spread across his chubby cheeks. But Sally pushed his hand away the second it touched hers and then she smacked that smug smile right off of his face.

"How could you wish us married?" Sally cried. "I don't even like you!"

"But you have to like me now, we're husband and wife."

"I don't care," Sally said. "I don't have to like you."

"Of course you have to like me!"

The pirate nodded his head. "If you wanted her to like you then you should have wished for that. Now you're going to have a loveless marriage that lasts forever."

The pirate laughed out loud and slapped his knee as Timmy frowned at his wedding certificate.

"Your turn, little lass," the pirate said to Sally. "If you want you can wish you never got married to him. How does that sound?"

Sally thought about it for a minute. She hated the idea of being married to the fattest kid in school, but if she used her wish to cancel out his wish then finding the end of the rainbow would've been a complete waste. It was her one chance to make a wish. It had to be something really good. She could always figure out another way to get out of being married to Timmy later on.

"No," she said. "I want to wish for something else."

"Well, what would you like?" the pirate asked.

She opened her mouth as if she was going to ask for the biggest, bestest wish anyone had ever wished in the world. But no words came out, pausing mid-breath. She had nothing in mind.

"I don't know yet…" she said.

"Well, you better hurry up. The rainbow is disappearing."

Sally looked up and saw the rainbow was indeed fading away. It was losing its solidity. The colors were beginning to blur.

"But I need more time," Sally cried.

"Just wish for something. Anything. Or you'll get nothing."

Sally gave herself just a second. The first thing she thought of was candy. She wanted all the candy in the world.

"I want..."

"Yes?" the pirate asked.

But then she looked around at the neighborhood around her. She was already able to get a piece of candy every day, but the kids who lived on the blurry side of town were lucky to get a single piece of candy each year. If she wished for all the candy in the world then they would get nothing. She wondered if she should make a wish that wasn't selfish. She wondered if she could make a wish that would stop the blurry kids from being sad all the time.

"I wish for..."

But then she thought it would be a waste if she didn't get anything out of it. She probably would only get one wish in her whole life and didn't want to waste it on other people.

"Yes, yes?" said the pirate.

Sally wondered if there was a wish she could make that would benefit both her and the blurry kids and everyone in the whole world.

The pirate sighed. "I'm sorry, but I have to go. It's now or never."

Sally opened her mouth, but couldn't wish. She just couldn't think of a perfect wish in such a short amount of time.

"Well, if you don't have anything you want..." The pirate walked over to the fading rainbow. "I'll be off then."

That's when Sally figured it out. She would wish for it to rain candy. If it rained candy then every child across the globe would be able to have it all year round. It would be absolutely free. All you'd need was a bucket to collect it and even the poorest of the poor could eat their fill of candy on every rainy day. It was the perfect wish.

But before Sally could make it, the pirate grabbed onto the end of the rainbow and was pulled up into the sky.

Sally ran across the park as fast as she could, running after the pirate as he went farther and farther into the air.

Then she yelled up at the heavens in as loud a voice as she could push out of her tiny lungs, "I wish it would rain candy forever!"

The pirate disappeared with the rainbow. Sally fell to her knees, right in the mud, not even concerned with getting her pretty yellow dress dirty. She didn't know if her wish was heard or granted.

Timmy pedaled over to her, looking up at the sky. "Did it work? Did you get your wish?"

Sally stared up at the clouds, waiting for it to rain candy. But nothing fell from the sky. She stayed there until the blurriness returned to the park.

"No," she said. "He didn't hear me..."

Then she stood up, wiped the mud from her dress, and punched Timmy in his plump arm.

"What was that for?" Timmy cried, rubbing the tender spot.

"That's for marrying me, you jerk."

She whistled at Stinky and the turtle flew back to her shoulder. Then she walked out of the park and wouldn't talk to Timmy on the way home no matter how close he followed her on his bike.

CHAPTER TWO

"What happened to your pretty new dress?" Sally's mother asked when she got home. Her voice was irate. It was almost always irate.

Sally shrugged and pushed past her.

"Why are you so late?" her mother asked.

Sally dropped her book bag on the couch.

"Are you wearing a wedding ring? Where did you get that?"

Sally shrugged again. She was too depressed about missing out on her wish that she didn't want to deal with her mother.

"I got married today," Sally said.

"What do you mean you got married?"

Then Stinky leapt from Sally's shoulder and flew around the room.

"Why is your turtle flying?" her mother asked.

Sally just went upstairs to her room.

"What the heck is going on?" Sally's mother said, dodging the turtle as it flew around her head like a bat.

When Sally got into her room, she changed out of her dress, exchanging her happy sunshine-yellow outfit for a dreary black and gray dress that she usually only wore at funerals whenever one of her dolls died and had to be buried in the backyard. She was in a funeral kind of mood that afternoon.

"What's wrong, Sally?" asked Mary Ellen, her favorite doll.

Sally frowned at her doll. "Nothing…"

Mary Ellen was like Sally's mini twin. She had curly black locks of hair just like Sally's and wore a frilly pink dress that Sally's mom made for her.

"You look down in the dumps," said Wendy May, the red-haired rag doll lying on her bed. "Did something bad happen at school?"

"No," Sally said. "I found the end of the rainbow today and was able to make one wish."

"What did you wish for?" Mary Ellen asked.

"I wished it would rain candy," Sally said. "But it didn't come true."

Sally sat down on her bed and five dolls came to her and snuggled against her like plastic puppies in little dresses. Nobody else in the family knew that her dolls were alive. It was a secret she had to keep from everyone she knew. Her dolls warned her that if she ever told anyone that they were alive then they wouldn't be her friends anymore. And that was worst thing that could ever happen to Sally. Her dolls were her best friends in the whole world. She didn't know what she'd ever do without them.

"How do you know it won't come true?" asked Mary Ellen.

"Because it hasn't rained candy yet."

"Just because it hasn't happened yet, doesn't mean that it won't come true." Mary Ellen hopped into Sally's lap. "I bet you the next time it rains there will be candy coming down from the clouds instead of water."

"Really?" Sally asked, her eyes filling with hope. "You think it's possible?"

"Of course it's possible!" said Mary Ellen. "You just wait!"

"Thanks, Mary Ellen."

Sally hugged her doll, feeling much better than she had before. She was hopeful that her wish could still come true. As she pulled away, the doll saw something shiny on Sally's hand.

"Where did you get this pretty ring?" Mary Ellen asked, holding up Sally's finger with both her hands.

"Oh…" Sally said, frowning at the diamond. "I got married."

"Married!" the dolls cried. "How exciting!"

"We must have a party to celebrate!" said Wendy May.

"We must have cake and presents!" said Flora, the bald baby doll with a missing left arm.

"But I'm not happy I got married," Sally said. "Timmy Taco, the fat kid next door, married me without my permission. It was what *he* wished for when we found the end of the rainbow." Mary Ellen pushed Sally's finger away. "Eww, I hate that kid! He's always running through the sprinklers in his underwear!"

"You can see his rolls of flab bouncing when he runs!" Wendy May cried.

Mary Ellen shook her plastic head. "You can't marry him. You just can't."

"But I can't get divorced," Sally said. "I'm stuck being married to him forever."

The dolls ran around in circles, yelling, "Gross! Gross! Gross!"

"He's not going to move in here, is he?" asked Baby Flora. "I don't want to share a room with that kid. He eats bugs and smells like Cheetos!"

Sally didn't think about that. Panic turned her rosy cheeks dark purple.

"I didn't think about that…" Sally held her mouth in her hand. "Husbands and wives are supposed to live with each other. What if my parents force me to live with him?"

The dolls jumped up and down in terror.

"Don't let him!" Mary Ellen cried.

"There will be Cheetos everywhere!" Baby Flora cried.

"He's so fat he'll break the bed!" cried a doll in a sailor outfit.

"We'll have to cut his throat in his sleep!" Wendy May cried.

"But then his body will stink up the place!" Mary Ellen cried. "This won't do at all!"

Sally spent the next hour calming her dolls and promising them that she would never let Timmy Taco live with them no matter what. She'd rather run away to another country where he'd never find her ever again.

Sally was in a foul mood all afternoon until her father came home. Whenever she was sad about something, her father was always the one who'd cheer her up no matter what was upsetting her.

Sally's father was her favorite person in the whole world. Not only was he the nicest father on the planet, he was also the biggest father anyone could ever have. He was like a mountain of beef and muscle, towering over all the other dads at the father/daughter picnic. Sally loved how he always wore the fanciest gray-plaid suits to work every day and had the shiniest gold-rimmed glasses. Whenever he gave her piggyback rides, she felt like she was driving a tractor or riding on the back of a massive grizzly bear. On his shoulders, she was so high in the air that it was like she was flying. She could touch the ceiling and reach high shelves that her older sister couldn't even reach with a stepladder.

"How's it going, Marshmallow?" her father asked, patting her on the head as he stepped through the front door.

Sally hated it when he called her Marshmallow, but she let him use the nickname anyway because she knew how much he liked calling her that. He said it was because of how soft and sweet she was.

After he asked the question, her frowning face expressed that things were not going well at all.

She said, "Timmy made me marry him today and when I wished it would rain candy nothing happened."

Her father didn't respond. He just leaned down and kissed her on the cheek with mint-stained lips, too excited to unwind after a long day at the office to concern himself with the child's fantasies.

Sally's dad worked as a stockbroker, but Sally didn't know what a stockbroker was. Whenever she asked him what his job was all about, he always told her that he made money for a living. Because of this, Sally imagined that he worked at a government factory printing dollar bills all day. It didn't seem like a very hard job at all.

"Did you bring me candy?" Sally asked.

Her father pulled out two Pixy Stix and Sally's frown exploded into a smile. Pixy Stix were her favorite.

"Save those until after dinner," he said, patting her on the head like a good dog. Then he pushed her out of his way.

When the father left the entry room, he saw the mother running around the family room with a broom. She was chasing after Little Stinky who'd just become the first turtle in history who refused to slow down.

"Stop it!" the mother cried as Stinky flew for the hallway.

The father stepped into Stinky's path and the turtle stuck to his chest like a suction cup.

"What the heck is this little guy doing?" the father asked, smiling down at Stinky.

"He won't stop flying everywhere!" the mother cried. "He already knocked over two vases and Grandma's urn!"

Before the father could grab him, Stinky hopped off of his chest and flew up the stairs.

"Well, isn't that something," the father said.

"You let him get away!"

"Turtles sure are livelier than when I was a boy," the father said.

When her parents turned to Sally for an explanation, she just frowned again. She was rather jealous that her turtle's wish came true but hers did not.

Jane didn't get home until dinner time. She was Sally's older sister, but Sally rarely ever saw her. Because she was a teenager, Jane preferred going out with her friends over staying home with the family. The only time she was ever around was to eat or sleep. She didn't even do her homework at home. She either did it at her friends' houses or just copied off the dorky guy who sat next to her during first hour.

"How was your day, Sunshine?" the father asked.

Jane plopped down in her seat at the end of the table. She didn't like the nickname her father gave her because it had been several years since anyone could have possibly described her as a ray of sunshine. She would be more aptly described as a gloomy cloud. With all her piercings and dark makeup, she looked like a soul-stealing witch who lurked in dark shadows awaiting her next victim.

Instead of answering her father, Jane turned to her sister and said, "Nice dress."

Sally's dark gray plaid dress was not much different than the one Jane was wearing. Jane was what she called a goth lolita, dressing in kawaii noir fashion that stemmed from her interest in Japanese culture. She and her friends spent most of their time at the bookstore in the mall, drinking coffee and reading manga while listening to Moon Kana, Strawberry Machine, and Kanon Wakeshima on their headphones.

"It's my funeral dress," Sally said with a smile, holding up a fork with a Swedish meatball on the end of it.

Her cheerful attitude did not match the style of her dress.

"Cool," Jane said. Then she swirled her plate of egg noodles with a spoon.

"You girls shouldn't wear such dark colors at the dinner table," the mother said.

"Why?" Jane asked.

"Because dark colors are depressing and off-putting. Good

girls always wear bright, happy colors like cantaloupe-orange or honeydew-green. Pink, baby-blue or purple would also be acceptable."

"I *am* wearing purple," Jane said, showing off her dark purple choker and matching wristlets.

The mother frowned. "That's not the kind of purple I'm talking about. If you wear purple it should be a lovely pastel violet. An Easter purple. Not a bruise purple. Your outfit makes you look like a bruise."

"At least I'm wearing a dress," Jane said. "You wouldn't let me wear pants and t-shirts like all the other girls at school, so this is my compromise."

Her mother waved away the argument with her glass of brandy. She was not accustomed to compromise.

She replied, "But I want you to be a proper lady. Girls are supposed to wear brightly colored dresses. A few centuries ago, you would've been burned at the stake for looking like that. Do you want to be burned at the stake?"

Jane rolled her eyes. Every day it was the same argument with her mother. It only made her want to dress even less conservatively. She couldn't wait until she was old enough to get tattoos. A skull tattoo right on her neck would be enough to send her mother through the roof.

"You act like a time traveler from the 1950s," Jane said. "If I dressed like you wanted me to I'd be a total nerd."

"Sally wears dresses and she's not a nerd," said the mother.

"She's only nine. Keep dressing her like that and people will think there's something wrong with her." Jane looked down at Sally. "People *already* think there's something wrong with her."

Sally frowned at her big sister. "I like my dresses."

The mother said, "Well, she's not going to dress like you when she's your age I'll tell you that."

The father cleared his throat until everyone looked at him.

"Well, I think both of my daughters look absolutely lovely just the way they are," said the father, towering over everyone at the table.

"You *would* say that," the mother told him.

"They can wear black or purple, dresses or pants, they can even wear a big bushy mustache dangling from the ends of their lips and I wouldn't mind one bit. As long as they're happy, that's all that concerns me."

The mother drank half her glass of brandy while glaring at the father. When she put her glass down, she calmly said, "It's because of that attitude she's got all that metal in her face."

"They're no different from the earrings you had since you were a little girl," said the father. "They're merely earrings for the nose, the lips, and the eyebrows."

"The nose ring makes her look like a bull," said the mother. "How can you stand by and allow your daughter to look like a bull?"

"And what is wrong with looking like a bull?" asked the father, smiling with his fork and knife pointed into the air. "A bull is a beautiful creature. It's proud and majestic. We should have paintings of bulls spread throughout the house to brighten up the place. I tell you, if more girls looked like bulls then no boy would be able to do anything but admire the beauty of the women around him all day long."

The mother pointed at the father's food, "Those meatballs on your plate were probably made from bulls."

"Mmmm." The father picked up a meatball with his fork and said, "They're even more beautiful in ball form." Then he took a bite and raised his eyebrows.

Sally laughed at her father. He was a very silly man. That was why she loved him more than anyone else in the whole world. He never raised his voice or argued with anyone. He never became upset no matter how bad things were. He was always cheerful and positive. Even when Sally broke her arm when she fell off the swing in first grade, her father was able to put a smile on her face and stay encouraging even when deep down he was terribly worried about her wellbeing.

Jane, on the other hand, was tired of her father's antics. She'd grown out of thinking he was cute and clever long ago. She was at that age where everything was very serious. Her music, her relationships, her art, her views on the world. These things were all very important. They *meant* something. She didn't know what they meant, but they meant something *deep* that was for sure. She did not have time for her father's juvenile behavior.

"You wouldn't guess what Sally did today."

The mother decided to switch attention from her eldest daughter to her youngest daughter. Dinnertime, for her, was not about bringing the family together. It was about giving her the opportunity to express her complaints with each and every member of the family in a situation where none of them were capable of running away.

"What did she do?" asked the father. "Cause caterpillars to instantly transform into butterflies just by being within her radiant presence?"

"No, worse than that," the mother cried, slurring her words. The mother's speech often slurred by the end of every dinner. It usually was when she decided to drink brandy instead of wine with the evening meal. "Besides teaching her turtle how to fly so that the vile creature would break all my vases, she also stole somebody's wedding ring and refuses to take it off."

Sally nearly jumped out of her seat when she said that. "I did *not* steal it!"

"Where did you get it then?" the mother asked.

"It's mine," Sally said. "I don't want it, but it's mine."

"Yeah, right," the mother said. "And how would a nine year old girl purchase such a ring?"

"I didn't buy it. It just appeared on my finger when Timmy married me. I can't take it off."

Jane grabbed Sally's hand and held up the ring.

"She's right," Jane said, tugging on the ring. "It really is stuck on her finger."

The mother pushed the butter tray down the table and told Jane to use that on it. "Grease up her finger and it will come right off."

The big sister did as her mother suggested, but the ring did not budge even a millimeter.

"It doesn't work," Jane said. "It seems to be embedded in her skin." She looked closely. "Actually, it seems to be a part of her skin."

The mother said, "That's nonsense." Then she went around the table to see for herself. She tried tugging with all her strength, intent on removing the stolen jewelry, even if it meant ripping her daughter's finger right off. She didn't let it go until Sally let out a high pitch scream.

"Don't be such a baby," the mother said, going back to her seat.

When Sally calmed down, rubbing her bright red finger, she said, "I've been trying to take it off all day, but it's useless. I'm stuck being married to Timmy forever."

"Who's Timmy?" the father asked with a big smile on his face. He was more entertained by the situation than anything.

"The fat kid next door," Sally said.

"Ah, the one who looks like a big bundle of dough," said the father, nodding his head. "The doctor's son. Yes, I know him well. He's a bit soft and squishy for a son-in-law, but he seems nice enough. Congratulations."

"I don't want to marry him," Sally said. "He's gross!"

"Then why'd you marry him?" the father asked.

"I didn't want to. When we went to the end of the rainbow today, we each got a wish. Stinky wished he could fly. Timmy wished we were married. And I wished it would rain candy forever."

"So that's why the turtle was so springy today," the father said, nodding his head with a meatball in his cheek.

"What are you talking about?" the mother said to Sally. "What do you mean you went to the end of the rainbow?"

"It was on the blurry side of town. There was this homeless

man there that said he would grant us each a wish."

The mother cried, "You went to the blurry side of town? You were speaking to strangers? You're so grounded, young lady!"

The father nodded his head at his daughter's story. "That must be some homeless man for granting your wishes."

"He said he was a rainbow pirate," Sally said.

"And you asked this strange man for candy?" the mother cried.

Sally shook her head. "I didn't ask him for candy. I asked for it to *rain* candy."

The mother was in a panic. "Did he do anything to you?"

"No," Sally said. "He didn't grant my wish at all. He granted Stinky's and Timmy's, but I wished too late. Now it's never going to rain candy."

"Don't be sad," her father said. "I'm sure your wish will come true."

"Really?" Sally asked.

"It'll rain candy one day, I promise."

"When?"

"Who knows. Maybe even tomorrow."

Then the father winked at Sally. The little girl quieted down and hid her smile under the table.

"Why are you humoring her?" the mother asked the father. "You're making her think it's okay to go to the blurry side of town and talk to strange homeless men. Who knows what that man had her do for that diamond ring she's wearing."

But the father ignored her. He just smiled at his daughter as he continued eating his Swedish meatballs, winking at her again when the mother wasn't looking.

"You're all a bunch of freaks, you know that?" Jane said to her family.

Then she stood from her seat and went up to her room.

CHAPTER THREE

The next day, Sally got up as early as she could. She jumped out of bed and rushed to the window. But when she tore open the curtain, hoping to see candy falling from the clouds, she saw nothing but a clear blue sky.

"Is it happening?" Mary Ellen cried, jumping up at Sally's knees. "Is it raining candy?"

Sally moped back to bed. "No…"

Mary Ellen followed her. All of her dolls hugged themselves to her body when she curled back into the covers.

"It's okay," Mary Ellen said. "It'll rain candy eventually."

"But when?" Sally asked.

"The next time it rains," Wendy May said.

Mary Ellen added, "You'll know if your wish will come true or not when it rains next. If it rains water you'll know the wish won't happen."

Baby Flora jumped in Sally's lap. "But if it rains candy, then you'll know it's true!"

Then Sally hugged Flora with all her strength. The dolls always tried to cheer her up whenever she was sad, because they knew whichever one cheered her up the most would get the biggest hug.

Sally got ready for school that day, putting on a bright blue dress with fancy puffball socks. She hugged her dolls goodbye, then got her lunchbox from the fridge and her book bag from the couch and went out the front door with a hop in her step.

"Bye, Mom," she called out, but she knew her mother didn't hear her. Whenever she drank brandy instead of wine the night before, Sally's mom always slept in late.

Sally took one step out the door and jumped as something smacked the cement beneath her feet. She bent down to see what it was. Lying there by her white open-toed shoe was a cinnamon candy. She picked it up, unwrapped it, and examined the red and white swirly globe. Then another piece hit the ground. This time a butterscotch. Then a few red vines. When something plopped into her curly hair, she pulled it out and saw that it was a tootsie roll. Within the next second, dozens of pieces of candy sprinkled down on her.

It was happening. She couldn't believe it. It was actually raining candy. She looked up with her mouth so wide that her lips cracked, hoping to see the clouds bursting with candy and showering from the sky. But that wasn't what she saw at all. Instead, she saw her father on the roof with a garbage bag full of candy. He was emptying it on top of her with a big smile on his face, sprinkling the sugary treats onto her like snowflakes.

"I told you it would happen," her father said with glee. "I told you your wish would come true and it would rain candy!"

Sally frowned. She was disappointed that it was only her father.

"It's not *really* raining candy…" she said.

"Of course it is! Look at this—it's a sprinkling of jellybeans! And this—a shower of sugar babies! A drizzle of dippin dots!"

He laughed like Santa Claus as he rained candy down on her. Sally appreciated her father's gesture, but it didn't cheer her up. She wanted it to rain candy so that all children all over the world would be able to have candy. She didn't want it to be a one-time thing just for her. Besides, anyone could make it rain candy like that. What she wanted more than anything was to experience the magic of having a wish actually come true.

"Thanks anyway, Dad," Sally said. "But it's not the same."

Then she grabbed five handfuls of candy from the ground,

stuffed them in her bag, and headed down the driveway.

"Have a good day at school, Marshmallow!" her father said, waving his arm and yelling so loud that all the neighbors could hear.

"How's it going, Wife?" Timmy Taco said on the way to school.

"I'm not your wife," Sally said, lowering her head as she walked.

Timmy pulled out the wedding certificate. "This piece of paper says you are."

Timmy was riding his bike alongside her, but was not pedaling as he moved. His legs dangled by the spokes, but for some reason the bike still moved. There was a new engine attached to the back.

"What happened to your bike?" Sally asked, pointing at the engine.

"My mom was tired of driving me to school every day, so she had this engine installed," he said. "Now I can go to *and* from school with you every day."

Sally didn't like that idea at all. She was always happy the fat kid was too lazy to ride his bike uphill in the mornings.

"Why don't you just pedal like normal people?" she asked.

Timmy was so embarrassed by the question he stuttered his words. "I have a medical condition. My leg got twisted and I pulled seventeen muscles last summer. The doctor said I shouldn't even walk on my leg for three years, but I do it anyway, because I'm really tough and can handle it. But I had to promise my mom I wouldn't strain myself while riding my bike, so I don't pedal. You know, because I'm not allowed."

Sally rolled her eyes. It was an unlikely story. All the out of shape children at school always had suspicious medical conditions to get them out of doing physical activity. Timmy Taco had become a master of making these kinds of excuses over the years. The only thing he hated more than having to do physical activity was being accused of not wanting to do physical activity. He had excuses for everything, even when it came to walking to the front of the class to solve math problems on the white board.

Trying to change the subject, Timmy said, "So I guess your wish didn't come true."

"No, but it will," Sally said.

"You really think so?"

"Next time it rains it will. You just wait and see."

Timmy nodded and then revved his engine to look cool. He didn't look cool.

"I hope so," Timmy said. "It would be great to have all the free candy I want whenever it rains."

"Oh, no..." Sally laughed. "With all that free candy you're going to get twice as fat."

"No I won't!"

"Yes you will."

Timmy became angry. "You can't call me fat. I'm your husband now. Wives aren't allowed to call their husbands fat."

"Who says?"

"My dad."

"Well, my mom calls my dad big and fat all the time and he's not even that fat. He's just really *big*. It's husbands who aren't allowed to call their wives fat."

"I would never call you fat," Timmy said.

"That's because I'm not fat."

"Well, I wouldn't call you fat even if you got fat."

"I won't get fat."

"You might if you eat all the free candy that rains from the sky."

"I won't eat it all at once. I'll save it for non-rainy days."

"Well, I still don't want you to call me fat ever again. It's embarrassing."

"Then lose weight if you don't want to be embarrassed."

"You're my wife now and you have to do what I say. I order

you to never call me fat again."

"I'll call you whatever I want."

"You have to eat lunch with me, hold my hand on the playground, and kiss me whenever I ask you to."

"I don't have to do what you say."

Timmy squinted his eyes at her. "You better if you know what's good for you."

When Timmy said this, Sally stopped in her tracks and glared at him. Just one look and Timmy's threat crumbled to pieces.

"Or what? You're going to hit me?"

"Maybe..." Timmy said.

Sally raised her fist. "Not if I hit you first."

"Girls can't fight boys," Timmy said. "They're too weak."

"Oh yeah?" Sally threw a fist into Timmy's face and paused a centimeter away from his nose. He flinched so much that he nearly fell off his motorized bike.

"But you're my wife now. My dad said that you'd have to do whatever I say."

"No, you have to do what I say," Sally said. "And I'm telling you to stay away from me. If you say anything to anybody at school about us being married then I'll punch you for real."

Then Sally walked away.

Timmy followed, riding alongside her, saying, "But they *have* to know. I've been waiting all night to tell everyone."

"I don't care. You tell anyone and you're dead."

"We can't keep it a secret forever. How are we going to hide these wedding rings on our fingers?"

"I'm keeping my hand in my pocket all day," Sally said. "You better do the same. And if anybody accidentally sees your ring finger, make something up. Tell them it's your new style. I don't care."

Timmy frowned. "But the wedding certificate..."

"What about it?" she said. "I'll never admit we're married to anyone. Even if you show the wedding certificate around the class, I'll say you forged it. I'll say your doctor father surgically implanted this ring in my finger to trick people into thinking we're married. You'll get made fun of by all the other kids for being a creep and your dad will probably go to jail."

Timmy didn't argue. He just looked at her with a sad expression. He wanted more than anything to be married to her. All night, he kicked himself for not making the right wish. He should've wished that she loved him or that she *wanted* to marry him. It wasn't satisfying at all being married to a girl who loathed him.

"Now stop following me to school," she said. "It's annoying."

Sally walked ahead, her puffy blue dress bouncing as she stepped.

All day at school, Sally looked out the window, watching for storm clouds. It was autumn and rain should've been very common, but the season was much drier than usual. It hadn't rained in weeks and the sky seemed as clear as summer.

"Pay attention, Sally," the teacher yelled at her, pulling her eyes away from the window. "You daydream far too much for a girl your age."

The teacher was a thick-figured woman named Mrs. Truck, who was so big and muscular that she rivaled Sally's father as largest adult in town. Sally couldn't tell if she was a masculine young woman in her twenties or a very athletic old woman in her fifties. The woman seemed ageless and genderless to Sally. She was like a powerful force of nature in human form, as if she was once a volcano or a tidal wave in a previous life.

"I wasn't daydreaming," Sally said. "I was just looking out the window."

The teacher flexed her bulky arm and pointed at six initials on the white board with a yardstick. They read M.O.M.S.E.F.

"Did you forget what this stands for?"

Sally hated the MOMSEF initials that were always printed on the top of the white board. Mrs. Truck made the class repeat the acronym twenty times on the first day of school and twice every Monday morning and afternoon since.

"Given that you've obviously forgotten, despite how many times we've gone over this, you must repeat after me." Then both Sally and the teacher said in unison: "Mind Open. Mouth Shut. Eyes Forward."

Sally rolled her eyes at the teacher. Mrs. Truck was very strict on her fourth graders.

"I expect all my students to MOMSEF at all times during class. If you can't MOMSEF, then you can't expect to pass. Now, will you MOMSEF, Sally?"

Sally just stared at the large woman for a moment. She hated how clever her teacher thought she was with that yardstick in her hand and that smug smile on her face. Coming up with that dumb acronym was probably her proudest achievement as a teacher.

"Yes," Sally said.

"Yes *what?*" the teacher asked.

"Yes, I'll *MOMSEF*," Sally said with her elbow on her desk, leaning her face against the palm of her hand.

Sally wished she could MOMSEF the teacher right in her fat face. Only her MOMSEF was an acronym for Millions of Mutilating Stabs Every Friday. It was only Wednesday, but on Fridays she would repeat the acronym in her head to cheer herself up whenever Mrs. Truck was being a pain.

"Well, Sally," Mrs. Truck began. She said this in the tone of voice she always donned whenever she was about to pick on one of her students. "Now that you're MOMSEFing, perhaps you'd like to come up to the board to solve the problem we've all been working on while you've had your head in the clouds."

Sally hated when Mrs. Truck called her to the white board. She always seemed to do it just to torture her. The large woman knew Sally wasn't paying attention and wouldn't be able to solve the problem, but the teacher hoped the humiliation of looking stupid in front of the class would motivate the young girl to MOMSEF more in the future. It was horrible logic, even for a teacher. A more effective method for teaching would be to make her lessons interesting enough to engage her students' attention, rather than terrifying them into submission.

When Sally was in the front of the class, the numbers on the board meant nothing to her. She was actually very far behind in her studies and Mrs. Truck was right that she really could've benefited by MOMSEFing more often, but she couldn't help herself. There were always far more interesting things to think about, or look at out the window, than Mrs. Truck's lectures.

Sally had to at least try, so she put the marker to the board and wrote random numbers in such tiny font and such sloppy handwriting that nobody would be able to read them. Then she stepped back.

"Are you finished?" Mrs. Truck asked.

"Yes," Sally said.

Mrs. Truck looked at Sally's answer but couldn't read it. This was Sally's way of getting out of solving problems on the white board. She hoped the teacher would get too frustrated trying to read the sloppy writing to deal with her and send her back to her seat.

"What does this say?"

"It's the answer," Sally said. "Can't you read it?"

"Of course not," the teacher said. "Who could possibly read such chicken scratch?"

"Well, am I right or not?"

The teacher squinted her eyes, trying to read the girl's scribbling. Sally knew it wouldn't get her out of looking stupid, but at least she was able to make Mrs. Truck look equally as stupid in the process.

"Is that a four or a two?" asked Mrs. Truck.

"What do you think?" Sally said.

Mrs. Truck couldn't tell one number from the other. They all bled together into a mess of scribbles.

"Just tell me the answer," said the teacher. "I don't have time to read your indecipherable scrawl."

Using her same tactic, Sally said the answer in such a mumbling incoherent voice that it didn't sound like anything. But she just wasn't clever enough to trick Mrs. Truck a second time. The teacher caught on to her game right then and there.

"You're lucky you're pretty, Miss Sandwich," said Mrs. Truck. "You'll need those looks to make up for that lack of a brain in your head."

All the other kids laughed and Sally's face went red. But they weren't laughing at her lack of intelligence nor Mrs. Truck's disparaging comment. They were laughing at Sally's last name. They always giggled and snickered when they heard her last name. Sally Sandwich was even more amusing to the children than Timmy Taco's name. There was also a child in the class named Bobby Burrito, but he was the school bully so nobody ever laughed at him even though it was a rather funny name. Sally, however, got more laughs than anyone. It was most likely because *sandwich*, if you think about it, is perhaps the funniest word in the English language. Even funnier than *hedgehog* and *pants*, which were the second and third funniest words, respectively.

For the rest of the day, Sally did her best to pretend she was staring at the white board. She wasn't actually paying attention though. She was just thinking about what it would be like if her wish came true and it actually did rain candy from the sky. Then all the other children would treat her like a hero instead of the dumb girl with the funny last name.

CHAPTER FOUR

For weeks, Sally watched the sky, waiting for it to rain. She had almost given up all hope until one Thursday afternoon in late October when she saw the first rain cloud in the sky. It was small and round and floating all alone like a marshmallow in a swimming pool. At first, Sally thought it was a blimp flying over their neighborhood, because it didn't look much like a cloud at all. It seemed to be made of rubber or plastic, and was bright white—even whiter than clouds usually got—with pink and blue polka dots covering it like confetti cake.

Later that day, the sky filled with more of the strange clouds. The other children in the neighborhood called them *circus clouds* and were very excited about seeing them in the sky even when their parents appeared clearly apprehensive over their presence. And it wasn't just happening locally. There had been sightings of such clouds all over the world, in Greece and Norway and Peru and even that small country off the coast of Africa that had only about 2,000 people living there. It was a most magical phenomenon that both thrilled and worried all the adults on the news stations. Only Sally Sandwich and Timmy Taco knew what they really were.

"It's going to rain candy!" Sally said to her dolls.

Her dolls were even more excited than Sally was, jumping up and down on her bed like chubby cartoon frogs.

Wendy May cried, "Yay! Your wish is coming true!"

"I told you it would!" cried Mary Ellen. "I told you it would come true, didn't I?"

"You sure did," Sally said.

"You have to bring us some!" said Baby Flora. "When it starts raining, bring us twelve garbage bags full of candy and spread it all over the bed!"

"Bring us so much we can swim in it!" yelled Wendy May.

"It will be most delicious, surely it will!" said Mary Ellen.

Sally ran down the stairs to tell her mother and Jane, who were already looking out the window at the odd clouds hovering over their house.

"Isn't it wonderful?" Sally asked.

"We've really done it this time," said the mother. "All the pollution we put in the air. The rain will surely be radioactive." Then she squeezed a fist until her knuckles turned white. "I knew I should've recycled more while I had the chance."

"It's got to be a trick of the light," Jane said. "Illusionists do this kind of thing all the time."

"Maybe if it was just one cloud, but this is happening all over the world."

Sally squeezed in front of them so they'd pay attention to her. "It's none of those things. My wish is coming true."

"What wish?" the mother asked.

"Don't you remember? I wished that it would rain candy. Those are candy clouds."

"Don't be ridiculous," the mother said.

"How else do you explain Stinky being able to fly?" Sally said. "His wish came true, Timmy's wish came true, and now my wish is finally coming true as well!"

Her mother shrugged her away, but Jane didn't dismiss her baby sister quite as easily. She was the only one who thought it was unexplainable how a diamond ring would become fused to Sally's flesh. They took her to the doctor a couple days after the incident and even the doctor couldn't figure out how it happened, nor could he figure out a way to remove it without amputating the finger. The mother just figured Sally did something really clever to trick even the doctor in order to keep that ring and not give it back to its proper owner.

"Is it really possible?" Jane asked. "If any clouds were going to rain candy they would definitely look like those."

"Don't you start now, too," the mother said.

"It's true!" Sally said. "Of course those are candy clouds! What else would they be?"

Then Sally ran outside before her mother could tell her not to.

"It's going to rain candy!" Sally yelled at the mailman as he walked down their driveway.

The mailman sorted a stack of mail in his hands as he walked, nearly running over Sally in his path. When he saw her hopping up and down, he smiled and then looked up at the sky.

"Candy, you say?" The mailman squinted at the clouds. "Now that would be something, wouldn't it? We could have all the free candy we could eat!"

Sally smiled up at the tall skinny man with the long chin. "I know! That's why I wished for it!"

Jane came outside, crouching down as she moved toward her little sister, as if standing straight up would be too dangerous beneath the supernatural clouds. The mother was too scared to go outside at all and hid in the living room, peeking through the blinds at her two daughters, waiting to see if anything bad would happen to them while out in the open.

"I think it's happening," Jane said to her sister.

She pointed at a few exceptionally bulbous clouds further in the distance. Over a neighborhood across town, they could see bits and pieces of things falling from the sky. They looked kind of like snowflakes but fell a lot faster.

"That doesn't look right," the mailman said, narrowing his

eyes at the distance.

"Is it candy?" Sally asked. "Is it really raining candy?"

Jane stood up straight and focused. She had really good eyesight compared to the other members of the family, but she still couldn't make out the details of the unusual rain.

"I can't tell," Jane said. "But it sure doesn't look like normal rain."

"It's probably just hailing," the mailman said, slightly nervous at the sight. Though it was just a rainstorm, it looked more frightening than seeing a tornado forming in the distance. "It hasn't hailed here in quite a while, but when it does it can get pretty big."

"Not as big as that," Jane said.

"It's raining candy, I just know it is!" Sally cried. "Lollipops and gummy bears and peanut butter cups and taffy and Pixy Stix!"

There were dozens of parents and children outside in their yards staring at the clouds, wondering what was going to happen next. The energy in the air could be felt even by young Sally. Everyone was anxious and mystified and just a little bit delighted that something magical was happening right before their eyes.

The first piece of candy fell on the driveway by Jane's foot. It was a green ball as big as a jawbreaker that shattered when it hit the concrete. The mailman went to the green spot and picked up a shard.

Sally stood on her tippy toes to look in his hand, "Is it candy? Is it really candy?"

The mailman tasted it. "It's sweet." He licked again. "It's lime-flavored." Then he popped it in his mouth and his eyes widened. "It really is candy!"

When he said those words, the smile on Sally's face stretched so big that it nearly swallowed her whole head.

Then another piece shattered on the other side of the driveway. It was also a round ball, but this one was orange. Sally ran to it, picked up every little sliver and shoved them in her mouth.

"It's orange cream!" Sally cried.

A blue ball clanked against the mail box. Then a pink ball hit the roof of the house. The next thing they knew it was sprinkling balls of candy all around them. They came in dozens of different colors and flavors, even spicy cinnamon, cola float and banana split.

"Yay!" all the children in the neighborhood cried.

Timmy Taco was next door, grabbing every piece of shattered candy he could find and shoving them down his shirt. Little boys and girls got down on their hands and knees, licking the colorful spots of candy dust on the sidewalk.

"Well, isn't this something!" the mailman said, throwing all the mail up into the air. "It's raining candy instead of hail! What a marvelous wonder!"

Then Sally and the mailman locked arms and danced in a circle, giggling at the magical miracle before them.

"Candy! Candy! Candy!" they sang, switching directions every three cheers.

It was the happiest moment of Sally's entire life, better than a hundred Christmases and birthdays combined. All the laughter and cheering of the children in the neighborhood was music to her ears. She had actually done it. She had brought joy to everyone.

But the moment did not last long.

Jane noticed it first. She heard the crying of the child across the street. A small boy lay on the sidewalk, holding his leg, screaming at the top of his lungs. Then Jane looked up into the sky. The light sprinkling of candy was turning into a hard rain.

"Sally, get inside," Jane said, stepping back toward the house.

A rock-hard chunk of candy the size of a golf ball landed on a garden gnome in their yard, shattering its ceramic head.

"Candy! Candy! Candy!" Sally and the mailman sang. They were too swept up in the moment to see what was happening.

"Get over here!" Jane cried.

The mailman stopped dancing and bent to the ground, picking

up a very special piece of candy.

"Look," the mailman said, holding up the candy chunk. "This one's rainbow-flavored!"

Sally was so excited to see it. It had all the colors of the rainbow in a single piece of candy. She held out her hand. "Oh, please let me have it!"

The mailman smiled and lowered it into her cupped palm. "Here you g—"

But the mailman froze in his spot before he could give her the rainbow chunk. His hand went limp and the candy dropped to the ground. Sally looked up at him to see blood streaming down his face and the life vanishing from his eyes. A piece of candy had hit him on the top of his head, falling as fast as a bullet, shattering his skull and piercing his brain.

They say that if you drop a penny from the Empire State Building it will instantly kill whoever it lands on. But these pieces of candy were falling from three times the height of the Empire State Building and were much heavier than one penny. They were basically small sugary meteorites.

"Sally!" Jane screamed. "Run!"

The mailman's body fell back, collapsing on the driveway. His blood oozed across the candy-speckled cement. And from there, the rain only got harder. The people in the neighborhood screamed, running for cover. The two young children across the street ducked into the dog house. Timmy Taco rolled into his garage, protecting his horde of sugary treats beneath his shirt. But not everyone was so lucky. Mrs. Jenson, two houses down, lay face-down on her front lawn. The fat man who ran the burger shop was missing his lower jaw from trying to catch a piece in his mouth. A speeding car swerved off the road and crashed into the Smith Family living room, filling the house with smoke and fire.

Sally couldn't move. She just stared at the chaos erupting around her. The wish was supposed to bring joy to people. It wasn't supposed to do this. It wasn't supposed to hurt anyone.

Jane raced across the driveway to her sister, picked her up by the waist, and ran back to the house. Sally didn't scream or say a word. She just looked back at the mailman's corpse lying in the driveway as it was buried in candy.

"Why did you go out there?" the mother yelled at her daughters as they burst through the door. "I told you it was dangerous. You could have been killed!"

Jane dropped her sister and then fell to the floor, gripping her arm. Sally looked down and saw her sister's blood all over her dress. She'd been hit by a falling blue sucker while carrying Sally to safety.

"What happened?" the mother cried. "What's wrong?"

There was a quarter-sized hole in Jane's upper arm. The piece of candy still stuck deep inside the flesh. Blood leaked down her fingers on the carpet. A shooting pain rippled across her arm and down her back.

"I was hit by one," Jane said, showing her mother the wound.

The mother backed away, disturbed by the sight. Her expression became angry, as if offended her daughter would show her something so disgusting.

"What did I tell you?" the mother said. "See what happens when you don't do what I say?"

"It's not the only one," Jane said.

She pulled down her gothic dress to exhibit three large welts on her back. The fluffy dress was enough protection to prevent the candy from breaking the skin, but she was surely going to have nasty bruises and maybe even a broken rib or two.

"We need to get her to a doctor," Sally said.

"We're not going out in this weather," the mother cried.

"Timmy's dad is a doctor," Sally said. "He's just next door."

"Fine." The mother sighed loudly and went to the phone.

"I'll see if he's home."

The mother was worried about her daughter but deep down she was also a bit pleased that something bad happened to her. *Serves her right*, she was thinking. Whenever any of her children broke the rules, she always prayed to God that something horrible would happen to them so that it would teach them a lesson and they'd actually start listening to her for a change.She didn't feel like rushing Jane to a doctor, even if the weather wasn't so dangerous, because she wanted her daughter to suffer just a little bit more so the lesson would sink in. She told her not to go outside—maybe not in words, but the message was clear—and that's what happens when you don't listen to your mother.

"The phone's dead," the mother told them.

Sally looked outside. Telephone lines were falling into the street. Trees were collapsing. Lightning struck like fireballs in the distance. For some reason, all the sugar and chemicals in the clouds caused the bolts of electricity to ignite. It was like there were dragons in the sky shooting flames at the houses below.

"He's probably at work anyway," the mother said.

"We should go check," Sally said.

"It's too dangerous," the mother said.

"You can wear thick clothes and use a metal cookie sheet as an umbrella," Sally said.

"I'm not doing that!"

"Well, if you don't I will."

"No, you won't!"

"I have to. This is all my fault."

"How is it *your* fault?"

"I was the one who wished it would rain candy."

"You think *that?* It's just a coincidence, you silly girl! This is obviously an act of God!"

As they argued, Jane lay on the ground between them, gripping her arm and squeezing her eyes as tightly as she could to block out the pain. Before the argument was over, the electricity

51

went out and the family went really quiet. They just stood there in silence, listening to the balls of candy pound against the roof overhead. It sounded like a thousand carpenters hammering the shingles to pieces.

The rain only got harder as the day turned to night. Sally stayed by the window, watching for signs of their father.

"When do you think Daddy will be home?" Sally asked every five minutes.

"He's probably dead," the mother said.

She was finally helping her eldest daughter, but not by going next door to acquire the doctor's services. She was trying to fix the girl up herself, using a pair of tweezers to pull out the candy stuck in Jane's arm. Candles burned on the table between them.

Outside, Sally watched the candy pile up in the street. It was deeper than any snowstorm they'd ever had, maybe three feet high in some places. It looked kind of like the ball pit at the kid's pizza party restaurant, only not at all as fun, especially with the dead bodies sticking out of it.

After a few hours of waiting, Sally's mother said, "Why don't you just go to sleep, Sally? He's probably not coming home anytime soon."

Sally looked up at her mother in the candlelight. "Do you really think he's dead?"

The mother didn't answer right away. Then she sighed. "I don't know. He probably got stuck somewhere. I'm sure he's fine."

Sally nodded in agreement. She hugged her older sister, then hugged her mom until she was pushed away. The mother didn't say another word to her.

"Goodnight," Sally said.

She went upstairs but she knew she wouldn't be able to sleep, especially knowing this disaster was all her fault.

"What's going on?" her dolls cried when she entered her room.

Sally sat down on her toy box and dropped her head to the ground.

The dolls scurried out of the dark like rats and curled around her ankles.

"It's so scary," said Mary Ellen. "What's happening?"

"My wish came true..." Sally said.

"We saw," Wendy May said. "It's raining candy."

"I didn't think it would be this way," Sally said.

"It's dreadful," said Baby Flora. "Free candy isn't worth any of this."

"Jane is hurt because of me, and the mailman was killed. I think a lot of people were probably killed."

"It's not your fault," Mary Ellen said, hopping into her lap. "You didn't know this would happen."

"But I should've made a better wish," Sally said. "I should've wished candy would grow from trees or was delivered in the mail every day. Now I'm a murderer."

The dolls giggled at Sally.

"A murderer?" Wendy May asked. "You're not a murderer."

"Yes I am," Sally said.

Mary Ellen asked, "Did you push the mailman into the path of that candy so that he would die?"

"No..."

Wendy May asked, "Did you wish to the rainbow pirate that the candy would kill people when it fell?"

"No..."

Baby Flora asked, "Did you stab a woman in the kidney with a serrated hunting knife and then twist it slowly clockwise until she blew her last desperate breath against your neck and fell limp into your arms?"

"No..."

"Then you're not a murderer, are you?" the cheerful dolls said in unison.

"I guess not..."

But the dolls didn't cheer Sally up like they thought they would. She couldn't help but take responsibility for what she wished for.

CHAPTER FIVE

Before Sally climbed into bed, a beam of shining light filled the street outside. She went to the window and saw a lone vehicle driving slowly down the road. It was her father's Range Rover.

Sally went downstairs and told her mother and sister what she saw, but the mother had polished off a whole bottle of brandy and was passed out on the couch. Jane had also been drinking to kill the pain, sitting alone in the dark, listening to music on her headphones.

"Daddy's coming," Sally said, pushing her sister until she snapped out of her foggy daze.

They went to the front window and watched as the Range Rover rattled down the road, climbing over the mountain of candy in four-wheel drive. The vehicle looked like it had been through a war. Dents and holes covered every inch of the exterior. The front and back windshields were so fractured that they could barely be seen through.

"It's really him…" Jane said.

"Of course it's him," Sally cried. "I knew he'd be alright."

The Range Rover pulled up the driveway, swerving around the mailman's mostly-buried body, through the yard, and parked as close as possible to the front door. Then the father stepped out and ran inside, avoiding the falling candy.

"Boy, is it raining hard out there or what?" the father said as he walked through the door, removing his broken glasses. "It's like cats and dogs, only twice as sweet!"

"Daddy!" Sally cried, running to her father and giving him a big hug. "You're alright!"

The father leaned down and kissed his daughter as he did every day. "Of course I'm alright."

When Sally looked him in the eyes, she saw something strange about his appearance. There was a mess of gore dripping from the side of his head.

Sally screamed at him. "Ahhh! What happened to your face!"

The father looked in the mirror at the gaping bloody wound. "Oh, this? It's nothing."

"You're missing half your face!"

"Certainly not," said the father, holding up a candle to get a better look. "I'd be dead if half my face was gone. This is more like a quarter at most."

The left side of the father's head had been stripped of skin, now the texture of blood-filled oatmeal. His ear was missing. His neck was torn apart.

"What happened, Dad?" Jane asked, looking carefully at his wound.

"Well, I couldn't see through the windshield while driving so I had to stick my head out the side window in order to know where I was going. I thought I'd be fine, but you know what? I got hit darned near fifteen times by that falling candy." He giggled and nodded his head. Seeing him giggle in his condition was a frightening thing. "Fifteen! Can you believe it?"

"Your skull's showing!" Sally cried, hiding her eyes behind her fingers. "You have to go to the hospital!"

"It'll be fine, Marshmallow," the father said, patting her on the head. She cowered from his touch. "I'll just get one of those Phantom of the Opera masks. Won't that be neat to have the Phantom of the Opera as your father?"

"No way!" Sally screamed and ran behind the couch.

The mother grumbled a few times in her sleep, but even Sally's screaming wouldn't wake her.

Jane and the father looked at each other for a moment. The

older daughter wasn't frightened of her father's wound, but she was concerned about him.

When he saw the wound on her arm, the father was more worried about her than she was of him. "Did you get an ouchie, too?"

"Yeah…" Jane said, holding out her arm. "I got a *big* ouchie…"

She pulled her arm away before he touched it, worried that he'd try to kiss it all better.

The father put the coffee table on his back for protection and trudged through the candy rain to the neighbor's house. He returned with a short bald man wearing rain boots and a raincoat over his pajamas. It didn't make sense that he was wearing rain attire when it wasn't the slightest bit wet outside.

"Hi, Mr. Taco," Sally said to the neighbor.

Mr. Taco was quite the opposite of his son, Timmy. He was not big and fat at all, nor was he the least bit lazy. Whenever Sally got up extra early in the morning, she would always see Mr. Taco running up and down the block in tiny spandex shorts and a sweatband around his bald head. She thought he looked awfully funny when he ran around, mostly because he raised his knees all the way to his stomach with each step and often ran in place whenever he got to stop signs. He had to be quite athletic to run like that, but he still looked rather silly. It was hard to believe that he was now Sally's father-in-law.

Mr. Taco greeted Sally and then went to her big sister. "Let me see here."

The neighbor sat down next to Jane and examined her arm. "This is a pretty nasty wound you got here, but I'll fix it up in a jiffy."

The father towered over the tiny doctor and said, "You might have to undo the damage my wife did trying to fix Jane up herself. I doubt she even sterilized those tweezers before she stuck them in her arm."

"*She* should be fine with the equipment I have," the doctor said. "But *you're* going to need to get to the hospital as soon as you can."

"Of course, of course," said the father. "But all I care about now is that my Sunshine is okay."

Jane glared at her dad. His cheerful behavior with half his face gone was obviously creeping her out.

Then she turned to the doctor. "Is the hospital even open?"

"Yes, but they're probably understaffed," said Mr. Taco. "They have generators, but with all the patients coming in it's probably a terrible situation. I would be there now if it wasn't for these roads."

"Will everything go back to normal tomorrow?" Jane asked.

Mr. Taco remained silent. Although he was an educated man and acted as though he were an authority on emergency situations, he knew even less than they did about the candy rain.

"Of course it will," the father said. "You just watch."

Mr. Taco spoke while removed the candy Jane's mother missed, "Even if it stops raining that stuff tonight we'll still be in a state of emergency for a few days. It'll take a while to repair all the damages the storm caused. Who knows when the city will be up and running again."

"At least I won't have to go to school tomorrow," Jane said.

"If the school's even still there," said Mr. Taco.

"What do you mean?" Jane asked.

"Some sides of town got it worse than others. On the radio, they said a lot of buildings have collapsed under the weight of that stuff."

Mr. Taco kept referring to it as *stuff* instead of candy, as if he didn't quite believe it was actually candy yet, or he was too scared to say it outright.

"If the school's there I doubt it's in one piece," the doctor said.

The father slapped Sally on the back, nearly knocking her to the ground. "You hear that, Marshmallow? At least that's some good news. No more homework."

Sally went to Mr. Taco. "How's Timmy? Is he alright?"

"Yeah, he's fine," Mr. Taco said. "He got a little bruise on his foot while trying to bring that stuff in from outside, but he's fine... He *will* be fine."

The doctor's voice went soft. There was something he wasn't telling her.

"How's Mrs. Taco?" Sally asked.

The doctor didn't respond, stitching Jane's arm in silence.

"Is she okay, too?"

The doctor kept quiet.

"Hey, Marshmallow," the father said. "Why don't you go upstairs? It's getting pretty late. It's well past your bedtime."

"But Dad..."

"Just go."

Sally decided not to kiss her dad goodnight, not with the wound on his face. She just backed away and went up the stairs.

When Sally was out of sight, she heard the neighbor answer her question.

Mr. Taco said to Jane and her father, "I was on the phone with her when it happened. She was leaving the grocery store and heading to her car. I didn't hear her cry out. I only heard the phone drop."

"That doesn't mean she was hit with falling candy," Jane said. "She might have been running for cover. And even if she was hit, she might have just been knocked out."

"I'm not worried about the stuff hitting her," Mr. Taco said. "She was in the parking garage. She was safe."

"Then why are you worried?" the father asked.

The doctor paused for a moment, putting his tools back into his bag.

Then he said, "Because of the gunfire."

"What do you mean?"

"I could hear it over the phone and I just knew..." the doctor's voice went hoarse. Sally couldn't see him, but she could tell he was crying. "On the radio, they said some psycho took a machine gun into the store and shot up the place. The police couldn't come. Most of the people couldn't escape, because of how dangerous the weather was." He paused again, collecting himself. "They speculate he was either some religious nut who took the rain as a sign of the end of the world, or he was just a malicious bastard taking advantage of the emergency conditions."

Both Jane and the father gave the doctor their condolences. They were very quiet after that.

"I haven't told Timmy yet," said the doctor, wiping his tears. "I don't even know *how* I'm going to tell him. He's got enough to deal with already. How do you explain this kind of thing to a child?"

Sally was crying as much as the doctor now. She couldn't hear any more of it. Timmy's mom was murdered and it was all her fault. If she didn't make that wish it never would have happened.

She ran to her room and buried herself in the covers, smothering her tears away with her pillows. The dolls crawled across her back and beneath her sheets, rubbing her skin with their plastic hands. But Sally ignored them. She blocked her ears with her pillows so tightly that she couldn't hear what the dolls were trying to say to her. But no matter how much she tried to block out all noise, she couldn't suppress the sound of the candy rain hammering against the roof of the house.

CHAPTER SIX

The next morning, the sound of hammering was gone. It had stopped raining. Sally jumped out of bed, knocking a pile of dolls onto the floor, and rushed to the window. Many of the polka dot clouds were gone from the sky. The sun was out, melting the candy in the streets.

"It stopped," Sally said. "It really stopped."

The fallen dolls rubbed their heads and stood up.

"That hurt, Sally," Mary Ellen said.

But Sally wasn't concerned with them at the moment. "Everything's better. Everything's going to be alright…"

Sally would've been more excited that the rain was over, but she couldn't feel relieved knowing it was all her fault. Her wish nearly destroyed the whole town, maybe the whole world.

She put on a white dress and snowshoes.

"Where are you going?" Wendy May asked.

Sally looked back at her dolls. The stiff plastic forms stood on the floor and on her bed, staring at her in the stripes of light that shone through her blinds.

"I have to see what I've done," Sally said.

"Don't go," Baby Flora said. "It's still dangerous out there."

"I need to see for myself what kind of damage my wish has caused. I hope it's not as bad as I suspect, but if it's even worse I have to know."

Then she left her dolls and went downstairs. Her family was still asleep. Jane and her mother were curled up into balls on each side of the couch. The father wasn't there. Sally guessed he was asleep in her parents' bedroom, but when she stepped outside she noticed his Range Rover was gone. She assumed he must have gone to the hospital once the rain stopped like Mr. Taco suggested.

The houses on Sally's street were all in terrible shape. The candy rain had shredded the rooftops into splintered, jagged messes. There were still pieces of multi-colored candy covering the houses, but most of it fell to the ground where it melted in the sunlight. Sally slugged through the sugary soup down the sidewalk, her snowshoes keeping her from sinking too deep in the colorful mud. She climbed over collapsed trees and stepped carefully around fallen power lines.

The neighborhood was silent. Sally felt as if everyone else was dead, as if she killed absolutely everyone in the town with her horrible wish. But then she realized that it was more likely that everyone was sleeping. During the whole ordeal last night, not a soul was able to sleep until the rain finally ended. Now, after it was all over, they probably dropped from exhaustion. They were probably deep inside comfortable dreams.

Sally came to one house that was in worse shape than the previous homes. In fact, it no longer looked like a house anymore. It was just a pile of rubble. Sally didn't know who lived there nor if anyone lived there at all, but she knew the house had a flat roof. The candy rolled off the houses with pointed roofs, but any home that enabled the candy to pile up was likely crushed under the weight of so many tons of sugar.

Farther down the street, the houses were in even worse shape. A fire had broken out and burned the buildings down. Because of last night's conditions, the fire department wasn't able to get out there to stop it from spreading. Some of the buildings were still smoldering.

But once Sally left the neighborhood and got onto the main road, it was a different scene altogether. Electricians were working on power lines. Construction workers were in bulldozers, clearing the candy out of the street. People were driving their cars, maybe returning home to their families or going out to help lend a hand in the crisis. It was a reassuring sight for Sally. The townspeople were putting everything back together again. Homes were damaged, people were hurt, but it wasn't the end of the world. It was just a normal disaster. No different than a tornado or a hurricane. After the adults cleaned everything up, life would go back to normal again and they'll have forgotten all about the candy rain.

These positive thoughts made Sally feel much better, but she still couldn't shake the guilt of what she'd done. If only her wish did *some* good for *someone*, then she would've been able to move on. That's when she thought about the blurry kids. They were so desperate for candy, surely they were happy that candy rained from the sky. Sally rushed across town toward the blurry neighborhood. She ran so fast that she slipped twice on the slick sidewalk and fell face-first into the candy mud. By the time she made it to the blurry side of town, her white dress had become a twenty-color splatter painting.

But once she arrived, she was not permitted to enter the blurry side of town. There was a roadblock in her path. A cop stood in front of her and held out his hand.

"Hold on, Missy," the cop said. "You can't go this way."

"But I *have* to go this way," Sally said.

The cop looked a bit like Sally's father after he returned home last night. There were wounds covering his face and hands. The officer must have been out all night trying to help people in town, hurting himself many times in the process. The helmet he wore was also dented in many places. It must have saved his life several times while he was out in the rain.

"Nobody's allowed in this neighborhood for the time being," the cop said.

"Why not?"

"Take a look around," the cop said. "If you think it's bad here it's twice as bad in there. They got it the worst."

"Well, when can I go in?"

"Not until they clear all the bodies away."

"What bodies?"

The cop sighed. He wished the girl would just go away so he wouldn't have to explain it all to her, but he found himself doing it anyway.

"Because of how blurry it is on this side of town, the people who live here didn't see what was falling from the sky. They probably heard something, but didn't realize the danger until it was too late. They couldn't even tell that other people were dying all around them as they stepped out into the street."

"But surely some of them stayed inside," Sally said.

"The houses aren't built very well in the blurry neighborhood," the cop said. "Not many buildings made it through the storm. Some people survived, but most of them were unlucky. It's a good thing it's too blurry in there to see the destruction clearly. I'm sure it would be a horrendous sight."

Sally didn't say anything more. She backed away from the blockade, shaking her head. At that moment, she realized she made a horrible mistake. She never should have gone out to see what damage her wish caused. It was far worse than she could have imagined. She would rather have not known for sure. She would rather have remained ignorant. She ran all the way home and didn't look back.

The father came home with his Range Rover full of food and supplies. He got Jane and the mother to help him carry it all into the house. Then he handed Sally a shotgun and a few extra shells.

"Hold onto this, Marshmallow," he said with a smile. "If anyone comes near the stuff in our truck you point this at them and yell for help."

The mother and sister were even more shocked than Sally.

"What the heck are you doing?" the mother asked, taking the shotgun away from Sally. "Where'd you get all this stuff?"

"The store," the father said, grabbing five bags of groceries at once.

"I thought the store was closed," Jane said, following after him with only one bag of food.

"It was," he replied.

The mother nearly fell over onto the candy-covered driveway when she heard him say that. "You mean you broke in? You *looted* the store?"

"Yeah," he said, placing the groceries inside the door and returning to the vehicle.

Judging by the untreated wound on her father's face, Sally assumed he never went to the hospital. He went looting instead.

The mother was so mad she nearly smacked him with the barrel of the shotgun. "You're going to get arrested! How could you?"

"Everyone else was doing it," he said.

"But why, dad?" Jane asked. "The rain stopped. Everything's okay now."

The father grabbed a gas-powered generator from the back.

"Haven't you been listening to the radio?"

"We don't have a radio," Jane said.

The father bumped his daughter out of the way as he moved the generator inside. "Well, on the car radio they said that the rain isn't going to stop any time soon. It stopped here, for now, but those weird clouds are still up there. They're all over the world."

"Are you kidding me?" the mother cried. "It's going to rain that stuff again?"

"You can count on it," the father said, handing Jane three gallons of gasoline. "And we need to be prepared."

As Jane carried the gas inside, she said, "But do we really need all this stuff? Guns? Gasoline?"

"Better to be on the safe side, Sunshine," the father said. "After we finish with this load, I'm going back for even more supplies. Who knows how long this disaster is going to last."

CHAPTER
SEVEN

The disaster lasted longer than anyone could have predicted. The scientists on the radio claimed that it would let up soon. They said there were signs of normal clouds returning and candy clouds dissipating. Although nobody actually saw these signs in their own skies, it was good news that gave everyone hope. It soon proved to be a bunch of lies, however. The candy rain was not going to end.

For six weeks, the town was in a state of emergency. They were hit by candy storm after candy storm. A local militia was formed to help the local police force. There was so much looting and violence between rains that the city needed as many men as possible to keep the peace. At first, the militia was helpful. They handed out canned goods to people in the neighborhood and helped reinforce rooftops to withstand the hard rains. But the more the candy fell, the more desperate and frightened people became. The militia soon went from assisting the police force to murdering the police force and taking over the town, keeping all of the city's supplies and resources for themselves. It was happening all over the country. Although the government was still in power, they were quickly losing control. It was all downhill from there.

The people might have been able to rebuild, might have been able to get things back under control, if it wasn't for one simple issue: there wasn't any water. Since it was only raining candy, it never rained the substance that all life on Earth needed to survive, causing a horrible drought to plague the countryside. Lakes and rivers were drying up. Wells and reservoirs were empty. All the water that evaporated into the atmosphere wasn't coming back down again. Instead, it was being transformed, by some magic, into candy. Some parts of the country were far worse off than others—Phoenix, Arizona for instance—but the drought would devastate every inch of the country eventually. Even the oceans would disappear one day.

With each passing day, Sally felt worse and worse. She thought of herself as the worst human being who'd ever lived. Worse than Hitler. Worse than Satan. She was the little girl who killed the world.

"It's not your fault," Mary Ellen said to Sally while she was having an exceptionally self-loathing day. "It was the fault of that nasty man who granted your wish. You didn't want it to rain *only* candy. You didn't ask him to make it stop raining water. *He's* the one who chose to grant your wish in such a devastating way. *He's* the one responsible for all this."

Sally grabbed Mary Ellen by the foot, ripped off both of her legs and threw her across the room. She was tired of her dolls trying to cheer her up. No matter what they said, it wouldn't change anything. Because of her the world was dying. She had to do something about it.

Sally ran outside and climbed up the mountain of candy that buried her family's house up to the windows. She looked up into the sky and screamed, "I wish it rained water again! I wish I never wished it would rain candy!"

She waited there, waiting for some kind of response from the heavens. She wished she could find that rainbow pirate again and force him to put everything back to normal.

"Come back, Pirate!" she cried. "Come back and grant me

another wish! I want just one more wish!"

But the pirate never returned. Because it didn't rain water, no more rainbows appeared in the sky. Without a rainbow, the strange man could not come back. She could never get another wish no matter what she did.

A piece of candy hit Sally in the back of the head.

"Ow!" she cried, rubbing her black curls—which were looking more like dreadlocks these days.

When she turned around, she saw Timmy Taco in his yard. He scooped up a handful of candy and threw them at her like rocks.

"It's all your fault!" Timmy cried. "You did this! You wished for this! I should have never married you!"

Sally covered her face to block the candy from hitting her. She didn't know what to say in her defense. Timmy was right.

"My mom's dead because of you!" Timmy cried. "All my friends at school are dead because of you!"

Timmy kept throwing the pieces of candy at her until he fell over in exhaustion. The kid had lost a lot of weight over the past six weeks. He was no longer the fat little boy Sally remembered. He must've been starving.

"I'm going to tell everybody what you did! I'm going to tell everyone you're the cause of all this! Then they're going to get you! You'll see! They're going to get you!"

When Timmy started throwing candy at her again, Sally ran inside her house and locked the door. That didn't stop Timmy from charging at their doorstep and yelling at her through the window. The once doughy child banged on the door until his knuckles were bloody, but he couldn't get in. Sally's house was well-barricaded. Her father made sure nobody would ever be able to get in or out unless he wanted them to.

"I hate you!" Timmy cried. "You're so stupid! It's all your fault!"

Then the boy stopped banging and screaming. He flattened himself against the outside of the door and slid down to his knees, crying his eyes out. Sally just listened to him on the other side. He was calling for his mother. He was begging her to pick him up from school and take him home with her. He didn't want to ride his bike anymore. He wanted to be with her as much as possible. He didn't want to follow the mean girl home or go with her when she chased after rainbows.

"Why all the gloomy faces?" the father said during dinner one night. "Cheer up. This might be the last good meal we have for a long time, so let's all enjoy it."

The three women in the family did not share his enthusiasm for cold beans. They had plenty of reserves to last them the last month or two, far more than the other families that were still alive in the neighborhood, but their stores had finally run out. It was the last of the food.

"What's the point?" Jane asked.

"The point is that beans are far more nutritious than candy, and candy's all we'll have to eat from here on out."

"Eww," Sally said. "I don't want to eat candy ever again."

"Candy is full of calories," the father said with a yellow-toothed smile. "No vitamins, but it will keep us going until we can find something better to eat."

Jane glared at her father. She stunk from lack of bathing. She was covered in bruises. She had absolutely no patience for the man whatsoever.

"I mean what's the point of going on living?" Jane asked.

The father smiled at her with a mouthful of beans, smacking his lips as he listened to her. The side of his head was more disgusting than ever, swollen in such a way that it was difficult for him to chew. He never did get to a hospital to have his face checked out, back when there still was a hospital. But being such a large strong man he was able to fight off the infection just by sheer will alone.

"Don't tell me you're going to give up on me, Sunshine," said the father. "We're not going to be one of those families like the Nelsons who commit group suicide just because they can't take a little hardship. We're survivors. We're going to get through this, just you watch."

"Get through what?" Jane asked. "It's the end of the world. There's no getting through this."

"Who says we can't? We're human beings. We'll find a way."

"We're just biding time until the inevitable."

As they argued, the mother ate one bean at a time with a fork and knife, savoring every microscopic taste. She was pretending that nothing strange was going on at all, that everything was perfectly normal. Sally was worried about her. She was getting scarier than when she used to drink.

"We will persevere," the father said. "I'll be damned if I let a simple disaster like this be the end of us."

"Dad, the human race has a year left, tops," Jane said. "That's what they said on the radio."

"I'm sure the government will figure something out."

"What government? The president was killed. The vice president shot himself. The only guy in charge is some general who doesn't give a shit about what happens to the majority of the civilian population."

"I'm sure the general knows what he's doing. He's probably got the top scientists in the country working around the clock in a secret bunker underground, trying to figure out a solution to this crisis."

Jane just couldn't stand her father's optimism. She considered herself a realist. Her instincts told her that at that moment, everyone left alive in the world were only out for their own survival. Even the people in charge. They didn't have a choice. The situation was too desperate to do anything else.

"Even if you're right and they do eventually solve this problem," Jane said. "Let's say they figure out a way to turn candy into water or stop the candy rain from happening all together. Even then, the world will never go back to what it used to be. It's too far gone. Why fight so hard for survival when there's no light at the end of the tunnel?"

"Of course there's a light," said the father, his smile still hanging on his lips. "There's always a light. There's even a light right now if you'd bother to see it."

"What light?"

"The four of us are together and enjoying a meal as a family. Isn't that something? If you ask me, it's a wonderful time to be alive."

"I haven't bathed in months," Jane said.

"It's a wonderful time to be alive!"

After a couple weeks of eating nothing but candy and drinking their own urine, Sally looked like a raggedy, pale-skinned walking corpse. The whole family did, except for the father who looked as big and meaty as ever.

"Well, I'm off hunting," the father said, leaning a hunting rifle over his shoulder. "Wish me luck!"

Every day he went off hunting for food and water. Every day he came back empty-handed.

"There's no food out there," Jane said. "The militia already picked everything clean."

"Then I'll hunt for birds and wild animals," said the father.

"The animals are all dead. Plants are all dead. There's nothing left out there but candy."

"I'll think of something, Sunshine. Don't you worry your pretty little head."

Then the father put on his metal-plated armor with a shield and pointed helmet—made out of street signs, cookie sheets, and parts of his Range Rover, all hammered into shape and stapled to leather clothing. It was good protection from both the candy rain and the roving gangs of cannibals that hunted by the highway.

When he left, the girls became uneasy. Although their house was well-barricaded, they didn't feel very safe when he was gone. Looters often came to the neighborhood to sneak into houses and steal whatever food they could find. Whenever these criminals came to their house, the father was always there to greet them with his terrifying size and half-mangled face. He would intimidate even a whole group of starving men into turning around and running off. But while he was gone, it wasn't so easy. The mother was useless, so it was up to Jane and Sally to scare them off with a shotgun, despite how pathetic and helpless they looked while holding it.

"Do you think anyone will come this time?" Sally asked.

They sat in the living room, watching their father through the window as he hiked over the candy landscape in his suit of homemade armor.

Jane shrugged. "People are getting desperate. There are more and more people out there every day."

"Their teeth are all rotting out," Sally said. "They eat nothing but candy so all their teeth are rotten."

"So are yours and mine," Jane said.

"Not as bad. We've had more real food to eat than most of them."

Stinky the turtle flew down from the ceiling and perched on Sally's shoulder, begging for food.

"I'm sorry, Stinky. I don't have any food for you."

The turtle licked her nose.

"All you have to eat is candy."

The turtle snuggled into her neck. It is what the turtle did whenever it wanted to persuade Sally into being fed.

"Here," Sally said, handing the turtle a sliver of green candy.

The turtle sucked it into its mouth and chewed on the candy. Then flew around the room. All that sugar made the turtle quite hyperactive. Sally was surprised the turtle was still alive. She figured he would have died days ago, since Father wasn't giving him a ration of water. It was good that Stinky didn't refuse to eat the candy or it would have had nothing to eat at all. She didn't know what she would do without her little friend Stinky. Watching it fly around the room was one of the few things she still enjoyed.

One morning, Sally smelled something wonderful coming from the kitchen. Ever since she began starving, Sally's sense of smell had become so intensified that she could smell one cracker from anywhere in the house. The smell woke her out of bed and she followed her nose all the way down into the dining room, where her mother was sitting, reading an old romance novel in her sweat-stained bathrobe.

"What are you eating?" Sally asked her mother.

The mother was eating spoonfuls of meat from a turtle-shaped bowl.

"Are you eating Stinky!" Sally cried.

The mother turned the page of her romance novel, then took another bite. Sally ran to the table with tears in her eyes.

"How could you eat my pet turtle?"

The mother wiped a tear from Sally's face and licked it off her finger.

"Don't cry," the mother said. "It wastes water."

"But… but…" Sally couldn't take her eyes off the turtle. It was a magical turtle. It could fly and everything. How could her mother do such a thing to such a beautiful creature?"

"I deserve to eat the turtle," the mother said. "It broke my best vases. This is payback."

"But your vases are worthless now! My turtle is worth more than ten thousand vases!"

"It would have died eventually anyway."

The mother flipped another page of the romance novel. She'd already read it a dozen times before. She knew the whole story by heart.

Sally couldn't take it. She hated her mother so much. She lunged at the remains of her pet and grabbed its shell.

"Give me back my Stinky!" Sally cried.

The mother grabbed her bowl, holding it in place.

"It's mine!" the mother screamed.

Tears showered from Sally's eyes. "You can't eat him! You can't!"

The mother grabbed a fork from the table and stabbed Sally in the cheek, then kicked her in the stomach until she fell to the ground.

"It's my food," the mother cried. "Mine! I caught it, I cooked it, I deserve to eat it!"

Sally didn't care about the pain. She curled up into a ball, blood trickling down her cheek, crying for her Stinky to come back to her.

"This is all your fault, anyway. *You* wished it would rain candy. If you weren't such a bad little girl none of this ever would have happened. You ruined everything."

Then the mother took her food and locked herself in the room. She never believed that Sally's wish actually did cause all this, even when all the evidence supported her claim. But she needed somebody to blame for her misery so she blamed the child.

Sally hoped she choked on the turtle.

Sally went upstairs, picked up the doll in the sailor suit, and pounded it flat with a hammer until its limbs fell off and its face was inside out.

"Why?" the doll cried in a mumbled voice. "Why?"

Sally had been taking her frustration out on her dolls for the past few weeks, cutting them, burning them, pulling off their limbs. She always apologized afterwards and put them back together as best she could, but it left them all looking charred, mangled and deformed. The dolls didn't seem to mind, though. Or if they did they didn't speak up about it. With those plastic faces, it was hard to know what they were really thinking.

When she finished with the doll, she sat down on the bed and screamed. Only Baby Flora came to hug her, wrapping around her with her half-burnt face and melted plastic arm. The other dolls hid under the bed.

"Why don't you play with us anymore?" asked Baby Flora.

Sally looked down at the doll. One of its eyes rolled into the back of its head, exposing the metal backside of the eyeball.

"I'm sorry..." Sally said. "I just don't feel like playing anymore."

"Why not?" Mary Ellen crawled out from under the bed. She was in the worst shape of all the dolls. Because she looked like Sally's twin, Sally abused her more than any of them. It was because she hated herself so much. Cutting, burning, and hammering Mary Ellen was Sally's way of punishing herself for being such a horrible person. "You used to always love playing with us."

"My mom ate my turtle," Sally said.

"But that's not our fault," said the doll with the inside-out face. "Why hurt us for something your mom did?"

"You should hurt your mom instead of hurting us all the time," said Baby Flora. "You should sneak into her room and cut off her foot. Then eat her foot in front of her like she did with your turtle."

"I can't do that..." Sally said.

"Sure you can," said Wendy May, hopping up onto the other side of the bed. "You just need a wood saw. Your dad has a saw, doesn't he?"

"No, no, no," Mary Ellen said. "A saw takes too long. She'll wake up after the first cut. What you need is an axe."

"An axe might not work either," said Baby Flora. "If you hit her over the head with a rock she'll be unconscious, then you can remove her foot in any way you want."

"And once her foot's gone, she won't be able to run away when you want to cut off another part of her!" said Wendy May.

Sally thought about it for a minute, then shook her head. "I'm not going to do that. She's my mom."

"We can do it for you," said Mary Ellen. "We'd absolutely love to teach that witch a lesson!"

Baby Flora and Wendy May jumped up and down, crying, "Yeah, let us do it! Let us do it!"

Sally shook her head.

"I don't want to talk about this anymore," Sally said.

"Then what would you like to talk about?" asked Mary Ellen.

The dolls didn't really care what they did or talked about when they were with Sally, as long as they were with her. Even getting beaten and burned by Sally was preferable to being without her. They weren't alive when Sally wasn't with them—they reverted back to normal lifeless dolls—so they tried to keep her with them as long as possible.

Sally said, "I want to try to figure out a way to save the world. I'll never be happy again unless I figure out a way to undo my wish."

"I'm sure there's a way!" said Mary Ellen.

"We'll figure it out eventually if we put our minds together!" said Wendy May.

"If I can get to the end of the rainbow again I'm sure I can undo my wish or wish all this never happened," Sally said.

Wendy May nodded her raggedy head. "Then that's exactly

what you should do."

"But there aren't any rainbows anymore," Sally said. "Without rain, there's no rainbows."

"Then you should make your own rainbow!" said Mary Ellen.

"How do I do that?"

"Well, rainbows aren't just formed when it rains. Remember how little rainbows are formed sometimes when the sprinklers water the lawn? You can do something like that."

"But nothing magical happens at the ends of those rainbows," Sally said. "They're too small. A rainbow pirate couldn't ride on one of those."

"Then make a bigger one," said Mary Ellen. "Find the biggest sprinkler system in the world and surely you'll make a rainbow big enough to meet the pirate again."

"But where am I going to get that much water? Where am I going to find such a sprinkler?"

"The government will help you," said Wendy May. "Talk to the president."

"I don't think there is a government anymore," Sally said. "There's a militia in town. They're the closest thing there is to government now."

"Then go see them!" cried Baby Flora. "Ask them for help!"

Sally nodded. She didn't think the local militia was going to have the resources to help her, but perhaps they would be able to find people who could. It was the only chance she had.

The next morning, Sally put on her hiking shoes and winter coat. It was now the cold season and the candy was frozen solid to the ground, no longer melting in the hot sun. When she was all bundled up, she snuck past her mother and older sister and walked the long walk out of the neighborhood. The place was more dead than she'd ever seen it. There was not a man nor dog nor bird in sight. There weren't even any ants eating the candy street. She figured ants would have been the most likely to survive the disaster, but without water even ants couldn't survive on candy alone.

She wondered how many people in the neighborhood were still alive. Most of them had died of thirst or killed themselves within the last month. She knew Timmy was still alive. He was no longer recognizable because of how skinny he was, but she often saw him shoveling candy in his yard or heard him crying for his lost mother. She knew Mr. Taco was getting small rations of food and water from the militia in exchange for his services as a doctor, but it probably wasn't much to live on.

The militia was set up at the old elementary school. It was well-fortified before the disaster with high walls designed to keep the children from running away or getting snatched up by stranger-dangers prowling the neighborhood in their windowless white vans.

When Sally arrived at the school, banners with the militia colors hung from every pole in the yard. The word MOMSEF was spray-painted on each wall of the building in big red letters. It was the name of the militia.

"MOMSEF?" Sally asked the guard standing at the gate.

She recognized the word. It had been hammered into her head every day at school. But it no longer meant what it did in class.

"That's right," the guard said. It was the same police officer Sally met at the blockade outside the blurry side of town. He was no longer a policeman, now a part of the local militia. "Do you know what that means?"

The guard had his assault rifle pointed at her. He wasn't nearly as friendly as he was when he was a cop, and his face was twice as scarred.

"It means Mind Open, Mouth Shut, Eyes Forward."

The guard looked at her with a confused face. "No, it doesn't."

"Yes, it does. Mrs. Truck said it does."

"You know Mrs. Truck?" asked the guard.

"She was my fourth grade teacher."

The guard nodded, lowering his gun away from her chest. "She's our leader now. MOMSEF stands for Military Officers Monitoring Safety for Every Family."

Sally was quite surprised to hear that her old teacher was running the local militia, but wasn't in the least bit surprised that she was still using her stupid acronym.

"We don't have any food for you if that's what you're here for," said the soldier. "If you've come to beg, you can just get lost."

"But if you're monitoring safety for every family shouldn't you be sharing your food with the rest of us?"

The guard laughed. "Maybe in the beginning, but we just don't have enough food to go around anymore."

"Well, I'm not here for food anyway. I need the militia's assistance with another matter. I have a solution for how to resolve the water crisis."

The guard smiled at the girl. He couldn't help but be amused with how official she was trying to sound.

"Oh yeah?" he asked.

"Yes," Sally said. "Unfortunately, it is all my fault this happened. I found the end of the rainbow and met a magical pirate who granted me one wish. I wished that it would rain candy."

The guard stared blankly at her.

She continued, "It's hard to believe, I know. But if we could create a rainbow using whatever water you had left, I might be able to find the pirate again and wish away my previous wish. In fact, if we're all together then you can all make wishes as well. Not only will things go back to normal, but you all can be rich or famous or whatever you want."

The guard couldn't believe what he was hearing. He shook his head.

"You live next door to the doctor, don't you?" asked the guard.

Sally nodded her head.

"The doctor's son was telling us the same story about you. He told us we should go to your house and murder you for causing all this."

Sally stepped back a little. She couldn't believe Timmy actually told them about her.

"Relax," the guard said. "We're not going to do anything to you. It's just funny that you two kids actually believe that story of yours."

"It's true!" Sally said.

The guard shrugged. "Maybe it is. It makes about as much sense as any of the other theories. But we're not going to risk any of our water to help you make another wish."

"What about the government?" Sally asked. "Can you get me in touch with whoever is in charge of the country? They might be willing to give me my idea a try. I'm sure they will."

"There's no government left, kid. We're all alone out here."

"But my sister said there was a general who took charge and is trying to find a solution to the disaster."

"Which one?" asked the guard. "There's been at least a dozen generals who took power since the president was murdered. What's left of the country has divided into thousands of small armies fighting each other over resources. And in other countries, it's even worse. The whole world's gone to shit."

"At least let me speak to Mrs. Truck. If I speak to Mrs. Truck I'm sure I can convince her."

"I can't let you see Mrs. Truck. She's a complete psychopath these days. She'd hang me from the flagpole if I came to her with this story."

"But what if I'm right? What if I could save us all?"

The guard sighed. "Look, kid. I want to believe you, I really do. It's just too far-fetched of a story. I'm willing to open my mind to the possibility if you could give me some kind of proof. If you can prove you actually made a wish that caused all this I'll let you see Mrs. Truck."

"What kind of proof?"

"Any proof. Did the leprechaun give you a pot of gold?"

"It wasn't a leprechaun. It was a rainbow pirate."

"Well, did he give you a chest of gold?"

"He said you have to out-swashbuckle him for his chest of gold. I don't know how to swashbuckle."

"Did he leave behind a magical pirate hat?"

"No, but he granted more wishes than just mine," Sally said. "My turtle wished he could fly. And it worked. My turtle could fly around the room like a bird."

The guarded nodded. "Very well. You show me this flying turtle and I'll believe your story. Even Mrs. Truck might believe it."

Sally frowned and lowered her eyes. "I can't. My mom ate it." Sally was even more upset with her mom at that moment. If only she hadn't been so mean, everything could have been fixed. "I still have its shell. I can bring you its shell."

"Unless the shell flies, it might as well be a normal dead turtle."

Sally lifted her ring finger to the guard. "Timmy wished that we were married. This ring appeared on my finger the second he made his wish."

The guard looked at the diamond. "It just looks like a normal ring to me, kid."

"It's not." Sally tugged on it. "No matter how hard you pull it, you can't get it off. It's a magic ring."

The guard looked at the ring more carefully. He could tell that it didn't look right on her finger. It seemed attached to the skin like it was a part of her, like she was born with it on her hand.

"That does look unusual," the guard said.

He flung his rifle over his back so he could use both hands to grab Sally's finger. He tugged on the ring, but nothing happened. He tugged again, using all his strength. Sally gritted her teeth at the pain, but endured it.

"You're right," said the guard. "It really is stuck on there."

The guard tried one more time, spitting on her finger to grease it up. While he was preoccupied with Sally, he didn't see the large figure coming out of the bushes behind him. Sally looked up and pointed, trying to warn the guard of the stealthy marauder. But it was too late. A thick arm wrapped around the guard's head and snapped his neck.

The large man who killed the guard was covered in weeds and camouflage paint. Knives and guns were strapped to his metal-plated chest. Sally didn't realize it was her own father until he spoke.

"Thanks for the distraction, Marshmallow," her father said as he lowered the dead body to the ground.

"Daddy?" Sally cried.

The father put his finger to his lips to hush her. Then he had her follow him as he dragged the body out of sight.

"Here, take this," he whispered, handing her the guard's assault rifle.

Sally held it more like a puppy than a weapon. "What are you doing here? Why'd you kill that man?"

"I've been trying to get in there for days," he whispered back. "They've got all kinds of food and supplies horded away. We're going to go in there and take it all for ourselves. We'll be set for months."

"What?" Sally cried.

He hushed her again.

"Don't worry," he said, looking back and forth to make sure nobody was coming. "I've been picking them off one by one. There's not nearly as many of them as there used to be."

"You're killing people?"

Her father patted her on the head. "Oh, these are bad people,

Marshmallow. They've been raiding people's homes and killing them for their food for the past month. We're only doing to them what they would have done to us."

"But Daddy—"

"Get down!" the father cried.

Then he pulled out a knife and flung it at another guard stepping outside the gates. The guard was only lighting a cigarette and didn't even see them coming.

"Let's move out," the father said, running toward the freshly killed guard to steal the rifle on his back.

Sally followed her father into the schoolyard, creeping along the jungle gym toward the building. They moved quickly but quietly, avoiding the guards who walked the perimeter.

"Now don't shoot them until you have to, Marshmallow. We don't want the noise attracting more guards." He pulled out a hunting knife and passed it to his daughter. "If you see one coming you should sneak up behind him, then stab him in the kidney and twist it really fast. I'll show you how."

Sally shook her head. She didn't need to be taught. Her dolls already showed her many times.

"I know how to stab someone in the kidneys, Dad."

"Good," he said, nodding his head. "That's important."

They crawled in through a classroom window. A woman was sleeping on a mattress on the floor. The father walked slowly to her, then covered her mouth and slit her throat.

As the woman's eyes opened, blood gushed out her neck, her screams muffled by the burly hand, the father said, "This is a good way to kill somebody in their sleep, but you have to make sure to cover their mouths when you do it. They still live for a whole minute while they bleed out and you don't want them alerting others."

The woman stared at the father with terror in her eyes, grabbing at his arm, as her life drained away.

Sally teared up as she saw the woman die. "But Daddy, she was just sleeping there. She wasn't doing anything wrong."

"But if she woke up, we would've been in big trouble," he said. "Always play it safe. It'll keep you alive in these hard times."

The father wiped the bloody knife on the mattress and stood up. Then he went to the door, opening it just a crack to see if the coast was clear.

"Come on," he whispered, then led her out into the hallway.

The militia kept their supplies in the cafeteria. The father got this information out of the principle of the school, who was in the bathroom relieving himself into a bucket when they crashed in on him. Sally wished she looked away sooner when her father drowned him in the bucket of his own waste. She was never very fond of the man, but thought even he deserved better than that.

"Be very quiet," the father said as they crept into the cafeteria.

There were about a dozen men and women in the room arguing with each other. Some of them were sitting at tables. The others were standing and pointing at each other as they yelled. Mrs. Truck was among them, yelling louder than anyone in the room. She was a massive sight to Sally. Unlike everyone else since the first rain, Mrs. Truck actually looked like she'd gained weight. She was larger and fiercer than anyone left alive.

"We can't just abandon them," said a scruffy man in a button up shirt. He was probably a lawyer before the crisis. Sally thought he had a good manner about him. "We have a responsibility to protect these people."

"To hell with them," Mrs. Truck yelled. "All we have to do is load up a truck and leave in the middle of the night while they're sleeping. By the time they wake up, we'll be long gone."

"But they're our friends," said a thin woman. "We can't do that to them. Those supplies belong to them just as much as us."

Sally and her father crawled along the outside of the tables, heading toward the kitchen. The people were so wrapped up in their discussion they didn't take notice.

"Besides, what are we going to do out there on our own?" the lawyer said. "Our numbers are what kept us alive this long. On the road, there's gangs of raiders and cannibals. How long do you expect us to live with just a dozen of us left? A week? A month?"

"Much longer than we would if we stayed here," said Mrs. Truck. "Trying to feed sixty-eight mouths with what we have left will be the death of us."

"Those guys are ex-military," the woman said. "If we try to get out of here they'll hunt us down."

"How?" asked Mrs. Truck. "Without water or gas, they'll be shit out of luck."

"Well, I won't stand for it," said the lawyer. "This is barbaric."

Mrs. Truck flexed at him. "What are you going to do about it, little man?"

"I'm going to tell everyone. I don't care if you're in charge. There's a lot more of us than there are of you."

"You're going to tell them, are you?" asked Mrs. Truck with that signature smug smile on her face.

The large woman pulled a revolver from her coat and shot the man in the face. The crowd gasped as his body hit the floor.

"You fucking bitch!" the woman cried, charging Mrs. Truck with a knife.

The fourth grade teacher shot her twice before she was stabbed in the stomach. Then all hell broke loose. The leaders of the militia took sides and started shooting at each other.

"Now's our chance," the father said to Sally.

Then they continued on.

As the gunfire echoed through the room, the two intruders

crept through the cafeteria into the kitchen. When they were no longer visible to the others, they stood up and ran to the storeroom. As the father opened the door, the smile fell from his face. There was hardly anything left, a mere fraction of what he expected to find. It was enough to keep the family going for a week, maybe a month if they spread it out.

"It'll have to do," said the father.

He loaded up a wheelbarrow with everything that he could, focusing mostly on the water. Then shoved packages of dried food down Sally's shirt.

"We have to move quickly," he said. "That gunfire's sure to bring others."

Before they could leave the kitchen, the shooting had stopped. Silence filled the cafeteria. Sally peered over the counter to see that only one person remained, standing like a barbarian over a pile of corpses. The teacher breathed heavily, covered in blood. As she wiped the sweat from her brow with the barrel of her gun, she saw Sally looking back at her.

"Miss Sandwich?" the teacher asked. "What are you doing here?"

Sally didn't mean to do it. The gun just went off. She was so scared that her muscles tensed up and her finger squeezed the trigger. Mrs. Truck had the dumbest look of surprise on her face as the bullets ripped through her chest. Sally always fantasized about murdering the mean old teacher one day, praying she could finally wipe that smug smile off her face for good. But after doing it for real, after seeing her guts spill out and her body crumple to the floor, she realized that murdering somebody was the worst possible feeling you could ever experience. Even worse than knowing that your wish was responsible for the end of the world. Sally felt so cruel and horrible at that moment that she thought about turning the barrel of the weapon on herself.

But there wasn't time to think for long. Sally's father grabbed her by the arm and pulled her out of the kitchen.

"Let's go," he said.

He doused the cafeteria with gasoline and set it ablaze. As the school burned, Sally's father led them through the hallways of smoke and fire, shooting down any man that got in his way.

"We can't let anyone see who we are," the father said, pushing the wheelbarrow as fast as he could. "Kill anyone who gets a good look at you."

But Sally couldn't do as he commanded. She stopped for one moment in front of an open classroom door and saw a whole crowd of people staring at her. The room was filled with women and children. Some of them were old classmates of Sally's. Bobby Burrito, the school bully, was there hugging his mother.

"Come on, move out," the father ordered when he saw his daughter stopped.

Sally just watched them for a moment. They didn't move or say anything. Based on the smoke pouring into the room, they obviously knew the building was on fire. But they didn't care. They had long stopped caring. The mothers hugged their children tightly, their eyes too dehydrated to cry. Every single one of them was ready to embrace death.

"Let's go!" the father shouted, continuing down the hall without her.

Before she continued after her father, Sally apologized to them. She told them it was all her fault. If she didn't make that wish none of it ever would've happened. But they didn't hear a word she said. They had died inside a long time ago.

CHAPTER
EIGHT

The food they'd killed so many people to obtain didn't last very long at all. It was hardly worth what they went through to get it. After a week, they were right back to surviving on nothing but candy.

"I can't do it," Jane said, pushing her plate of rainbow-colored sugar away. "I can't eat anymore of this shit."

Even though they only had candy to eat, they still sat at the dinner table for their evening meal. It was the worst part of the day for everyone except the father. The dinner table brought back too many memories of all the big home-cooked delicious meals they used to have. Even the memory fast-food nights made their mouths water.

"Me neither," Sally said, pushing her plate away. "I'll never eat another piece of candy ever again."

The father ate his candy with a spoon and fork, pretending it was the most appetizing food he'd ever eaten.

"You just have to use your imagination," said the father. "Instead of candy, pretend it's a scrumptious bowl of children's cereal. Like that Flintstones one. Fruity Pebbles."

"I hate Fruity Pebbles," Jane said.

"You used to *love* Fruity Pebbles," said the father.

"Yeah, when I was three."

"Well, pretend it's something you do like. Pretend it is stuffed bell peppers."

Jane threw the bowl across the room and screamed, "I'm not pretending it's anything!"

"Jane!" the mother yelled when she saw the bowl fly. She stood up and slapped her eldest daughter across the face. "Not my good dishware!"

"Who cares about your fucking dishware?" Jane yelled.

"I do! I care! It's not like I can go buy a new set at the store."

"You're both a couple of psychopaths!"

During the family outburst, the father kept silent. He stared forward, deep in thought. When Jane and her mother were finished yelling at each other, he took a deep breath. Then he pushed his bowl away.

"Very well," he said. "If this isn't good enough, I'll go find us something better to eat."

Then he got up from the table, put on his shoes, and went for the door. He returned an hour later, carrying a slab of meat over his shoulder. He plopped it onto the table.

"We're having meat tonight," the father said.

Sally's eyes lit up. It had been ages since she'd had fresh meat.

"Where'd you get this?" the mother asked.

"Who cares where he got it," the mother said, grabbing the meat and taking it to the fireplace.

"I hunted it down," said the father. "It wasn't moving very quickly, so I didn't even need to waste a bullet.

"What did you hunt?" Jane asked. "There aren't any animals still alive out there."

The mother stuck the meat onto a metal skewer and placed it on the fire. It was the closest thing they had to a stove.

"Who said it was an animal?" the father asked.

The whole family paused for a moment. Jane's mouth dropped open.

"Are you saying that's human meat?" Jane asked.

"Of course it is," said the father. "That's actually Mr. Taco from next door. So I guess you can call it taco meat." Then the father chuckled at his little joke.

After learning that it was human flesh in the fireplace, the mother hesitated for a moment. But only a moment. Once her stomach got the best of her, she went right back to preparing the meal.

"You killed Timmy's dad?" Sally cried.

The father nodded. "He was scavenging through some houses a few blocks away. The poor guy must've been pretty starved. He was eating baking powder right out of the box. Just handfuls of baking powder." The father chuckled.

"I'm not eating Mr. Taco," Jane said. "You're sick. You're completely insane."

The smell of cooking meat filled the room.

"You should have seen the look on his face when I invited him to dinner. To *be* dinner, that is. It was priceless."

"How could you?" Jane said. "He was your friend. He helped me when I was wounded."

The father smiled and rubbed Jane's head.

"Oh, don't worry so much about it, Sunshine. He would've died anyway. He wasn't cut out for this style of life."

"But what about Timmy?" Sally cried.

"We'll get Timmy later, Marshmallow. We've got enough of Mr. Taco to last us a while. The rest of him is being preserved out in the cold."

After the meat was cooked, the mother cut it into pieces and served them on nice plates.

Then she told her daughters, "Your father already killed him. We might as well not let him go to waste."

"Are you really going to eat it?" Jane asked her.

The mother lifted her fork and knife. "Just pretend it's pork roast."

The father picked up the meat with his hands and took a bite. As he chewed, he nodded his head at the mother's words. "That's the right attitude. Waste not, want not. This will be just the food we need to get us through the winter."

Sally looked down at the meat on her plate. She couldn't believe her father killed Mr. Taco of all people. Timmy already lost his mother. He was going to be devastated when his father didn't return home.

"Go on, Sweetie," the father said, pointing his fork at the meat. "Eat up."

Sally didn't know what else to do. She was so hungry, she couldn't just let it go to waste. But when she took her first bite, all she could think about was the nice bald man next door who used to run past her house every morning in his tight spandex shorts and dorky sweatbands. It took every ounce of her willpower to swallow each bite.

In the end, even Jane couldn't fight her hunger. She closed her eyes and ate the slab of meat faster than anyone else at the table. Then went to the fireplace for more.

When they finished eating what was left of Mr. Taco, the father grabbed his assault rifle and went out to hunt for more. Sometimes it took a couple days, but in the end he always came back with pack full of more meat. The mother would be ready to cook it up on the fireplace and the children did everything they could to pretend they were eating pork roast instead of human flesh.

"No matter how hard I try, I can't find that fat kid from next door," said the father. "He must have died or ran away."

"I'm not eating Timmy," Sally said.

"Why not, Marshmallow?" the father said, then the shimmer of the diamond on her finger caught his eye. "Oh, yeah. He's your husband now, isn't he? Well, maybe instead of eating him we can invite him to join the family. We could use another man to help with the hunting."

"Timmy doesn't know how to hunt," Sally said.

"That's okay," said the father. "I can teach him. I can teach you, too, if you like."

Sally shook her head.

A storm came into town and showered the house with rock-sized chunks of candy. It was the worst they'd ever been through, and the sugary bits piled up so high, the front door couldn't be opened. For days, the father couldn't go out on hunts so he stayed at home with his family. Jane was extra cranky when the father was around. The mother was even more cranky when she wasn't being fed.

"What do you think of my new hunting outfit?" the father said, showing off a robe made of human flesh and bone.

Because he wasn't able to go outside in the storm, the father used his time stitching together a new horrifying suit of armor. There were skulls for shoulder pads, rib bones sticking out of the armbands like spikes. His helmet was a collection of human faces sewn together, their mouths and beard hair still attached.

"You look like a monster," Sally said.

"Exactly." The father smiled, turning back and forth like a fashion model, showing off the details of the stitching along his thigh. "I'm hoping to inspire fear in my prey. They won't think clearly when they're afraid."

"It's so disgusting," the mother said.

The father smiled again. The mouths on his flesh mask were also smiling. He stitched them up to look that way.

"Don't feel left out," said the father. "I made one for each of you."

He pulled a box out from behind the couch and lifted the flesh outfits so they could see them. Then he passed them out, saying, "One for Sally, one for Jane, and one for the most lovely woman a man could ever have."

The women held the outfits as far away from their bodies as they could.

"Go on, see if they fit," said the father.

Sally looked at hers and cringed. Her outfit was made from other children her age. She thought she recognized one of them.

"I don't want to wear it, Daddy."

"But you have to," the father said. "Soon this whole area is going to be empty of prey and we'll have to move on to better hunting grounds. When that happens, we're going to need to look like a terrifying gang of cannibals that even other cannibals will be too frightened to mess with."

The father had them all put on their flesh costumes, then lined them all up in front of the mirror.

"See, look at how ferocious we look?" the father said.

He wrapped his arms around his girls and let out a heart-warming sigh, basking in the view of his beloved family, imagining what a great family photo that would've made. Then he kissed Sally on the top of her head.

"Merry Christmas, Marshmallow," the father said.

Sally pulled the flesh hat out of her eyes.

"Merry Christmas, Daddy."

Sally found her older sister dead in the upstairs bathroom a week later. She'd cut her wrists and bled out. After everything that had happened to them, she just couldn't take it anymore. She couldn't spend one more moment with her father and his horrifying outfits. She couldn't eat one more serving of someone else's flesh.

The mother didn't hesitate for a second. She didn't shed a single tear. She just picked up her dead daughter's body and cut her into steaks for their next meal.

When Sally sat at the table, wearing her suit of bones and flesh, she just stared at the meat on her plate. This was far worse than even the first time, when it was Mr. Taco. As she stared at the food, all she could think of was all the time she'd spent with her sister, all the arguments she used to have with the rest of the family. She missed her more than anyone else who had died.

"Eat your sister, Marshmallow," the father said when he

realized she hadn't touched her plate.

Sally looked up at her father. He slurped up the meat on his plate as if it were a normal chunk of meatloaf the mother had picked up from the store. She knew it was better to eat her sister than kill somebody else for the meat, but she couldn't believe how easy her parents were able to do it. She wondered if they would react the same way if it were she who had died.

"I can't," Sally said. "I miss her too much."

The father said, "I miss her too, Sweetheart. But we have to move forward. A lot of horrible things happen in times like these. We can't be too sentimental."

"But you act like you don't even care that she's dead."

"Of course I care," the father said, taking another bite.

Sally looked down at her plate. She still couldn't believe that her sister was gone.

"I miss her," Sally said. "I wish she was still alive."

The mother and father nodded between bites.

"I want to kill myself, too," Sally said.

The father removed the flesh helmet from his head and set it down on the table. Then he stared her in the eyes. For the first time in as long as Sally could remember, her father took on a very serious tone.

"Don't you say that," the father said, pointing at her. "Jane was weak. You're strong. She couldn't take it anymoreand gave up. You're not going to do the same. You're going to make it. You're going to survive longer than anyone else in the world. You just watch."

Sally nodded her head.

"Now finish your dinner and then go up to bed."

When the father took another bite, he chomped into something hard it chipped his tooth.

"What is it?" the mother whined at her husband's cringing face.

The father dug his finger into his mouth and pulled out a piece of metal.

"Eyebrow ring," he said.
It made a clinking noise when he tossed it on his plate.

CHAPTER
NINE

"We can kill him for you," Wendy May told Sally when she lay in bed that night. "We can cut his throat and watch him drown in his blood."

Sally rolled over. She didn't want to talk about killing her own father. He had become a monster, but Sally knew that he did so only out of love. It required a monster like him to protect a child like her in times like these.

"He won't hate you," said Baby Flora. "He'll probably respect you for it. That's exactly what he's doing to other people. I bet he'd be proud."

"I know he would," said Wendy May. "You just watch."

Sally covered her head with her pillow. She didn't care what her dolls said, she wasn't going to hurt him. The visions of when she killed Mrs. Truck still plagued her thoughts. She couldn't imagine what would it would be like if she killed her own father, even if it was her dolls who did it.

"You don't need either of your parents," Mary Ellen said, hugging Sally's back. "You have us. We're all the family you need."

Baby Flora snuggled between her legs. "You can get rid of both of them. Then you won't have to lock us in the room all day."

Wendy May said, "We can go into the living room. We can go anywhere we want."

"We can play together forever," said Mary Ellen.

The dolls then hopped excitedly on the bed. "Forever! Forever!"

"Wake up, Marshmallow," the father said, barging into her room at the crack of dawn. "It's time to go hunting."

Sally rolled over to see her father standing in the doorway in his hunting outfit.

"Get dressed," he said. "We leave in an hour."

"I don't want to go hunting," Sally said.

"You have to. It's an important skill you're going to need to learn if you're going to survive. I won't be around to provide for you forever."

As Sally got out of bed, her dolls rolled onto the floor, unmoving, pretending to be normal not-living dolls.

"But can't I just stay home with mom?" Sally asked.

The father shook his head. "After all that's happened, I think it would be better for you to keep your mind occupied. Now put on your hunting clothes and meet me downstairs."

Sally wished she was putting on a pretty dress like her mother used to buy her, but what she had to wear was not pretty at all. She squeezed herself into the leather outfit and stared at herself in the mirror. The eyeless faces in her outfit stared back at her.

"You look absolutely stunning," Wendy May said.

Sally looked down at the raggedy doll and said, "No, I don't."

Downstairs, her father was collecting supplies for the trip. They needed plenty of guns, knives, ammo, rope, and some Jane jerky, as the father jokingly referred to it, for hunting rations.

"What's the rope for?" Sally asked.

"Ah, a good question," the father said. "A good question, indeed. The rope's very important for many different things. You can use it to set snares and tie extra supplies to your back, if you find anything useful along the way, but what it's best for is when you have to take prisoners."

"Prisoners?" Sally asked.

The father nodded. "Sometimes you might find a small child while you're out there, but small children are not good eating at all. They have hardly any meat on them. But where there's a child, you're sure to find a grownup close by." The father held up the rope to demonstrate. "So you want to tie up a child as tightly as you can to a street sign or a bike rack in the middle of the town. Then you cut off a toe. Just a little toe, to get the kid screaming. You don't want him to bleed to death before anyone comes. Then you sit back and wait for someone to come."

"Do people really come?"

"Always," the father said. "Every single time!"

"But what if the kid's parents are dead," Sally said. "Won't you be waiting around for nothing?"

"That's the beauty of it!" the father cried. "Even if the child has no parents, somebody still comes. You see, adults can't help themselves when it comes to helping a child in need. The child could be a total stranger, and they still feel a deep instinctual urge to help them. It's part of their biological makeup. Even the biggest, meanest thug in the whole world will come to a child's aid. I guarantee it! And once they come, I sneak out of my hiding spot and shoot them down lickety-split. That's how you turn an appetizer into a grand feast!"

As the father handed her a backpack and an assault rifle, Sally realized it was going to be very difficult hunting with her overexcited father. It sounded like a gruesome experience. She didn't know how she was going to get through it.

"But you'll see how it all works soon enough," said the father, putting his gear onto his back and his flesh helmet on his head. "You'll get lots of hands-on experience, you can count on that."

Sally looked back at her mother standing in her robe by the fire, but the woman didn't say a word. She just stared at her daughter and husband in their morbid outfits and waved them goodbye, waiting for them to get back with the next meal.

"See you soon, my dear," the father said, as he opened the front door. "Keep the fire going for us."

As the father turned and took one step onto the candy-covered ground, a gunshot rang out. Sally saw the blood explode from her father's chest. He looked down at the bullet hole in his leathery outfit and tumbled back. Then he dropped his gun and fell to his knees.

A half-dozen men ran down the driveway toward them, raising axes and machetes, screaming like wild banshees. Sally helped her wounded father inside, then shut the door.

"What's going on?" the mother screamed as the men banged on the door outside. "What do they want?"

Sally put both hands on her father's wound to keep the blood inside. "What do you think they want?"

"They're hunters." The father coughed blood. "You have to get out of here. Go out the back."

Sally didn't do as he commanded, keeping pressure on his wound.

"No, no, no, no!" the mother cried.

"I'm sorry, Marshmallow," the father said, staring into his daughter's eyes through his gruesome mask. "I should've known this would happen. I should've prepared you better."

The sounds of wood chipping apart as they hacked at the front door with angry axes, hooting and hollering like wild man-beasts lusting for blood.

"It was the fire," said the father. "They probably saw the smoke from the chimney. I'm such an idiot. I should've known." He grabbed his shotgun. "Go on. I'll hold them off."

Sally let go of the wound and blood gushed into the air.

Then she backed away, grabbing her assault rifle.

"Come and get it," the father said.

He fired the shotgun through the door, blowing one of the marauders in half. The blast killed one, but also created an opening big enough for them to break through. Before the mother and daughter could get a chance to run, the men were already inside.

The first man through the door swung a sledgehammer at the father's head. The cracking sound made Sally fall to the ground as she watched her father's jaw snap in half and his teeth shatter across the tile floor. The other men jumped over the father and charged straight for Sally's mother. She just screamed as they threw her to the ground.

"Get away, get away, get away!" the mother cried, punching with her frail little fists.

A man with his teeth rotting out of his head smiled crazily at Sally and licked his wrinkled cracked lips at her. As he ran for her, Sally raised the machine gun and pulled the trigger. The sound was like a burst of a chainsaw, tearing the marauder's guts out. Once he fell, Sally pointed her gun at the man with the sledgehammer, who raised the mallet high over his head to finish the father off.

When Sally pulled the trigger, the flurry of bullets shredded the living room furniture and family photos on the wall. It wasn't until she discharged the last few rounds that she blew the top of the man's head off. He dropped the sledgehammer and fell limp onto her unconscious father.

A muscled man with long gray dreadlocks tore the rifle from Sally's hand and clubbed her in the face with it. She dropped back and everything went dizzy. Blood oozed from her nose. The room started spinning.

"Mommy..." she said, her voice sounding like it was underwater.

She reached out her hand with slow motion as she saw the two men grab her mother by the hair and drag her across the floor into the next room.

"Mommy…" Sally said. Her own voice seemed distant, but her mother's screams seemed even further away. There was a loud ringing in her ears.

The man standing above her unbuckled his pants and pulled them down to his ankles. She turned her head away from him to look at his father who was trying to get back to his feet. His jaw dangled from his face like a raw steak. But he was out of it even worse than Sally. The man with no pants walked over to the father and buried a hatchet in his skull. Then he went back to Sally.

The girl hardly knew what was happening as the man with the dreadlocks pulled off her hunting outfit and removed his underwear. As he lowered a knife to Sally's throat, a small black form jumped on his shoulder and stabbed him in the back of his neck.

"Death to the intruders!" Baby Flora cried.

All of Sally's dolls hopped down the stairs, jumping on top of the horrible man. They had little razor-sharp knives that they'd been hiding in Sally's sock drawer, and used them to cut the man's flesh everywhere they could reach.

"Kill him! Kill him! Kill him!" Wendy May, the rag doll, yelled as she went straight for his jugular.

"Make him a woman!" cried Mary Ellen, who sliced off the ugly piece of dangling meat between the man's legs.

"Die! Die! Die!" the other dolls said, hacking at his legs and ankles.

As her dolls went to work on him, Sally smiled and giggled with glee.

"You did it," she said to her dolls. "You saved me."

But then the dolls faded from Sally's eyes. The man descended on top of her with not a scratch on him. Sally had long forgotten that her dolls were only a figment of her imagination. They seemed so real to her for so long that she thought they really could talk, that they really could save her from these horrible people.

Sally disappeared for a while. Her mind faded into the back

of her head. But only for a moment. Not long after, she was thrown back into consciousness by the sound of a shotgun blast. Then the big ugly dreadlocked head of the man lying on top of her exploded like a red juicy cantaloupe.

When she crawled out from under the body, she saw Timmy Taco standing there, holding her father's shotgun. He was not imaginary like her dolls. He was all skin and bones, as skinny as a skeleton with paper-white skin, but it was really him.

Another man came running out of the other room and Timmy blew him away—the shotgun blast forming a crater of gore in the man's chest. The force of the blast threw Timmy's weak body to the ground, but he pulled himself back up and moved forward. He walked cautiously into the next room fired one last shot. Then he came back out again, dropped the gun on the floor, and went back home next door without saying a word.

Everything was silent except the ringing in Sally's ears. She pulled herself to her feet, covered herself with a couch cushion, and looked around her living room. The bodies were motionless. The floor was covered in blood.

She expected at any minute her father would stand back up and say, "Boy, that sure was a pickle we were in, wasn't it, Marshmallow?"

But his body was just as dead as the rest of them.

Sally was too sore to walk very quickly. She took one step at a time, limping into the next room. Her mother lay on the dining room floor, naked, her legs spread apart with a dead man lying on top of her. She wasn't moving. Based on the red marks on her throat, Sally assumed that she was strangled to death. She liked to think it finished quickly, hoping her mother didn't suffer too much. Her mother was always such a wimp when it came to pain.

Upstairs, Sally put on a dress. The same sunshine-yellow dress she wore when she made that wish all that time ago. Her dolls lay on her bed, not moving, not speaking. They never spoke to her ever again after that.

When she walked next door, Timmy was sitting on his couch, flipping through an old photo album.

Sally came in and sat down next to him. He was obviously irritated by her presence, but she didn't care. She couldn't be alone after what had happened.

"I saw you," Timmy said, breaking the silence.

Sally looked up at him.

"Saw what?"

"I saw you eating my dad," he said. His voice was calm and quiet. "I was there when your father killed him. I followed him back to your house. I watched through the window as he fed him to your family."

Sally looked away.

"I didn't want to eat him…"

Timmy turned the page in the photo album.

His voice wasn't very upset. Either he'd long since come to terms with what had happened or he was completely dead inside.

"I don't care if you wanted to or not," he said. "You still did it."

Sally's voice softened. "I'm sorry…"

"All this is your fault," he said. "You never should have made that wish."

"I know."

"It was so stupid. It was the worst wish anyone's ever had."

Sally nodded slowly.

They sat there in silence for a while. Timmy flipped through his photo book, touching the images of his parents with his finger, remembering all the smiles and hugs and happy times they spent together.

Sally had the itchy feeling that they weren't alone. She felt as though the neighborhood was full of people, all of them hiding in the shadows, waiting for the moment to jump out to get them. She imagined dozens of marauders following those that attacked her house. The feeling told her to get out of there, quickly. Leave Timmy and run, hide, get to safety as soon as possible. But she didn't want to run. She didn't want to hide. So she just stayed where she was, sitting next to Timmy.

"Timmy?" Sally asked.

"Yeah?" he said.

"Why are you still alive?" she asked. "How did you survive all of this time?"

He shrugged. "I don't know."

"You haven't been killing people like we did."

"Of course not," he said.

"Then what have you been eating?"

"Nothing," he said.

"Not even candy?"

He shook his head.

"I don't understand."

"I don't understand, either."

"I haven't had an food or water for weeks."

"Shouldn't you be dead?"

He closed his book of photos and looked back at her.

"Yes, I should," he said. "I *wanted* to die. Even before my father was killed, I stopped eating because I wanted to die."

"Then, how…"

"The wish," Timmy said. "If you stopped eating it would be the same thing. I don't think either of us can die of thirst or starvation. I don't think either of us can die at all."

"What do you mean?"

He held up his ring finger. "I wish we would be married forever."

Sally looked at her own ring, then back at him. "Yeah, so."

"Well, you know the line, '*Til Death Do Us Part*,'" he said. "If we were to die we would no longer be married. But I wished that we would be married forever. In order to be married forever, we have to live forever."

"So we can't die?"

"That's what I'm saying."

"Never?"

"Never."

She just stared forward with her mouth wide open.She couldn't believe it.

"That's impossible," she said.

"So is candy rain," he said.

"We can't live forever," she said. "The world is over. What are we going to do?"

Timmy shrugged.

"We're going to have to stay here, for all eternity, on this dead candy-covered planet?"

"And you thought your wish was bad," he said.

The feeling that thousands of marauders were coming to get them suddenly disappeared from Sally's mind. Now a new feeling overwhelmed her thoughts. She now felt the opposite. She felt that they were completely alone. Outside of their house, the streets were deserted. The city they grew up in was a ghost town, occupied only by the cold sugary wind. She felt that the countryside beyond their town was nothing but a desert. And beyond that the nation was a wasteland. The oceans were dried up. The whole planet was just one big candy-covered graveyard.

The two of them, sitting on the couch, were all that was left. And they would still be there long after even time itself had come to an end.

BONUS SECTION

This is the part of the book where we would have published an afterword by the author but he insisted on drawing a comic strip instead for reasons we don't quite understand.

I hope you liked my new book *Sweet Story*. Wasn't it just splendid?

It's me CM3!

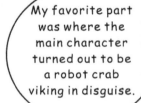

My favorite part was where the main character turned out to be a robot crab viking in disguise.

A what?

just finished reading it

Then he jumped over that tanknado on his lazer bike.

Umm...

FACT: A tanknado is a tornado but it's full of tanks

Look, I barely met the deadline for Sweet Story as it was. I just didn't have enough time to write a new comic. You don't know how hard it is to come up with these things for every book.

How hard can they be? I know six year olds who can draw better comics than this in less than an hour. You didn't have a spare hour?

I didn't even have a spare minute! I was waaaay too busy assassinating the emperor of the Imperials for a Dark Brotherhood quest in Skyrim.

You didn't make a new comic because you were playing Skyrim?

In Skyrim, I am Darkwort the Deadly, a level 30 wood elf assassin! Harbinger of the Companions! Eater of dragon souls! And my stealth bow attacks can kill an ice troll in one hit!

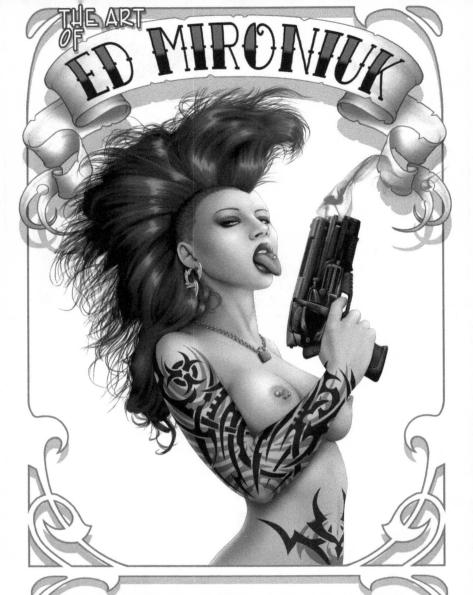

ABOUT THE AUTHOR

Carlton Mellick III is one of the leading authors of the bizarro fiction subgenre. Since 2001, his books have drawn an international cult following, despite the fact that they have been shunned by most libraries and chain bookstores.

He won the Wonderland Book Award for his novel, *Warrior Wolf Women of the Wasteland*, in 2009. His short fiction has appeared in *Vice Magazine, The Year's Best Fantasy and Horror #16, The Magazine of Bizarro Fiction,* and *Zombies: Encounters with the Hungry Dead*, among others. He is also a graduate of Clarion West, where he studied under the likes of Chuck Palahniuk, Connie Willis, and Cory Doctorow.

He lives in Portland, OR, the bizarro fiction mecca.

Visit him online at **www.carltonmellick.com**

Bizarro Books

CATALOG   SPRING 2013

ERASERHEAD PRESS

Your major resource for the bizarro fiction genre:

WWW.BIZARROCENTRAL.COM

Introduce yourselves to the bizarro fiction genre and all of its authors with the Bizarro Starter Kit series. Each volume features short novels and short stories by ten of the leading bizarro authors, designed to give you a perfect sampling of the genre for only $10.

BB-0X1
"The Bizarro Starter Kit" (Orange)
Featuring D. Harlan Wilson, Carlton Mellick III, Jeremy Robert Johnson, Kevin L Donihe, Gina Ranalli, Andre Duza, Vincent W. Sakowski, Steve Beard, John Edward Lawson, and Bruce Taylor.
236 pages $10

BB-0X2
"The Bizarro Starter Kit" (Blue)
Featuring Ray Fracalossy, Jeremy C. Shipp, Jordan Krall, Mykle Hansen, Andersen Prunty, Eckhard Gerdes, Bradley Sands, Steve Aylett, Christian TeBordo, and Tony Rauch. **244 pages $10**

BB-0X2
"The Bizarro Starter Kit" (Purple)
Featuring Russell Edson, Athena Villaverde, David Agranoff, Matthew Revert, Andrew Goldfarb, Jeff Burk, Garrett Cook, Kris Saknussemm, Cody Goodfellow, and Cameron Pierce **264 pages $10**

BB-001 **"The Kafka Effekt" D. Harlan Wilson** — A collection of forty-four irreal short stories loosely written in the vein of Franz Kafka, with more than a pinch of William S. Burroughs sprinkled on top. **211 pages $14**

BB-002 **"Satan Burger" Carlton Mellick III** — The cult novel that put Carlton Mellick III on the map ... Six punks get jobs at a fast food restaurant owned by the devil in a city violently overpopulated by surreal alien cultures. **236 pages $14**

BB-003 **"Some Things Are Better Left Unplugged" Vincent Sakwoski** — Join The Man and his Nemesis, the obese tabby, for a nightmare roller coaster ride into this postmodern fantasy. **152 pages $10**

BB-005 **"Razor Wire Pubic Hair" Carlton Mellick III** — A genderless humandildo is purchased by a razor dominatrix and brought into her nightmarish world of bizarre sex and mutilation. **176 pages $11**

BB-007 **"The Baby Jesus Butt Plug" Carlton Mellick III** — Using clones of the Baby Jesus for anal sex will be the hip sex fetish of the future. **92 pages $10**

BB-010 **"The Menstruating Mall" Carlton Mellick III** — "The Breakfast Club meets Chopping Mall as directed by David Lynch." - Brian Keene **212 pages $12**

BB-011 **"Angel Dust Apocalypse" Jeremy Robert Johnson** — Meth-heads, man-made monsters, and murderous Neo-Nazis. "Seriously amazing short stories..." - Chuck Palahniuk, author of Fight Club **184 pages $11**

BB-015 **"Foop!" Chris Genoa** — Strange happenings are going on at Dactyl, Inc, the world's first and only time travel tourism company.
"A surreal pie in the face!" - Christopher Moore **300 pages $14**

BB-139 **"Hooray for Death!" Mykle Hansen** — Famous Author Mykle Hansen draws unconventional humor from deaths tiny and large, and invites you to laugh while you can. **128 pages $10**

BB-140 **"Hypno-hog's Moonshine Monster Jamboree" Andrew Goldfarb** — Hicks, Hogs, Horror! Goldfarb is back with another strange illustrated tale of backwoods weirdness. **120 pages $9**

BB-141 **"Broken Piano For President" Patrick Wensink** — A comic masterpiece about the fast food industry, booze, and the necessity to choose happiness over work and security. **372 pages $15**

BB-142 **"Please Do Not Shoot Me in the Face" Bradley Sands** — A novel in three parts, *Please Do Not Shoot Me in the Face: A Novel*, is the story of one boy detective, the worst ninja in the world, and the great American fast food wars. It is a novel of loss, destruction, and--incredibly--genuine hope. **224 pages $12**

BB-143 **"Santa Steps Out" Robert Devereaux** — Sex, Death, and Santa Claus ... The ultimate erotic Christmas story is back. **294 pages $13**

BB-144 **"Santa Conquers the Homophobes" Robert Devereaux** — "I wish I could hope to ever attain one-thousandth the perversity of Robert Devereaux's toenail clippings." - Poppy Z. Brite **316 pages $13**

BB-145 **"We Live Inside You" Jeremy Robert Johnson** — "Jeremy Robert Johnson is dancing to a way different drummer. He loves language, he loves the edge, and he loves us people. These stories have range and style and wit. This is entertainment... and literature."- Jack Ketchum **188 pages $11**

BB-146 **"Clockwork Girl" Athena Villaverde** — Urban fairy tales for the weird girl in all of us. Like a combination of Francesca Lia Block, Charles de Lint, Kathe Koja, Tim Burton, and Hayao Miyazaki, her stories are cute, kinky, edgy, magical, provocative, and strange, full of poetic imagery and vicious sexuality. **160 pages $10**

BB-147 **"Armadillo Fists" Carlton Mellick III** — A weird-as-hell gangster story set in a world where people drive giant mechanical dinosaurs instead of cars. **168 pages $11**

BB-148 **"Gargoyle Girls of Spider Island" Cameron Pierce** — Four college seniors venture out into open waters for the tropical party weekend of a lifetime. Instead of a teenage sex fantasy, they find themselves in a nightmare of pirates, sharks, and sex-crazed monsters. **100 pages $8**

BB-149 **"The Handsome Squirm" by Carlton Mellick III** — Like Franz Kafka's *The Trial* meets an erotic body horror version of *The Blob*. **158 pages $11**

BB-150 **"Tentacle Death Trip" Jordan Krall** — It's *Death Race 2000* meets H. P. Lovecraft in bizarro author Jordan Krall's best and most suspenseful work to date. **224 pages $12**

BB-151 **"The Obese" Nick Antosca** — Like Alfred Hitchcock's *The Birds*... but with obese people. **108 pages $10**

BB-152 **"All-Monster Action!" Cody Goodfellow** — The world gave him a blank check and a demand: Create giant monsters to fight our wars. But Dr. Otaku was not satisfied with mere chaos and mass destruction.... **216 pages $12**

BB-153 **"Ugly Heaven" Carlton Mellick III** — Heaven is no longer a paradise. It was once a blissful utopia full of wonders far beyond human comprehension. But the afterlife is now in ruins. It has become an ugly, lonely wasteland populated by strange monstrous beasts, masturbating angels, and sad man-like beings wallowing in the remains of the once-great Kingdom of God. **106 pages $8**

BB-154 **"Space Walrus" Kevin L. Donihe** — Walter is supposed to go where no walrus has ever gone before, but all this astronaut walrus really wants is to take it easy on the intense training, escape the chimpanzee bullies, and win the love of his human trainer Dr. Stephanie. **160 pages $11**

BB-155 **"Unicorn Battle Squad" Kirsten Alene** — Mutant unicorns. A palace with a thousand human legs. The most powerful army on the planet. **192 pages $11**

BB-156 **"Kill Ball" Carlton Mellick III** — In a city where all humans live inside of plastic bubbles, exotic dancers are being murdered in the rubbery streets by a mysterious stalker known only as Kill Ball. **134 pages $10**

BB-157 **"Die You Doughnut Bastards" Cameron Pierce** — The bacon storm is rolling in. We hear the grease and sugar beat against the roof and windows. The doughnut people are attacking. We press close together, forgetting for a moment that we hate each other. **196 pages $11**

BB-158 **"Tumor Fruit" Carlton Mellick III** — Eight desperate castaways find themselves stranded on a mysterious deserted island. They are surrounded by poisonous blue plants and an ocean made of acid. Ravenous creatures lurk in the toxic jungle. The ghostly sound of crying babies can be heard on the wind. **310 pages $13**

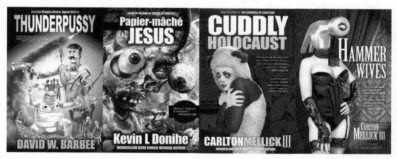

BB-159 **"Thunderpussy" David W. Barbee** — When it comes to high-tech global espionage, only one man has the balls to save humanity from the world's most powerful bastards. He's Declan Magpie Bruce, Agent 00X. **136 pages $11**

BB-160 **"Papier Mâché Jesus" Kevin L. Donihe** — Donihe's surreal wit and beautiful mind-bending imagination is on full display with stories such as All Children Go to Hell, Happiness is a Warm Gun, and Swimming in Endless Night. **154 pages $11**

BB-161 **"Cuddly Holocaust" Carlton Mellick III** — The war between humans and toys has come to an end. The toys won. **172 pages $11**

BB-162 **"Hammer Wives" Carlton Mellick III** — Fish-eyed mutants, oceans of insects, and flesh-eating women with hammers for heads. Hammer Wives collects six of his most popular novelettes and short stories. **152 pages $10**